CHASING MY TWENTIES

Charleston, SC
www.PalmettoPublishing.com

Chasing My Twenties

First Edition

Paperback ISBN: 979-8-218-95505-2
eBook ISBN: 979-8-8229-2427-7

CHASING MY TWENTIES

A Journal Series

AMANDA BERUBE

Introduction:

I'VE ALWAYS BEEN INFATUATED WITH THE IDEA OF KEEPING A CONSISTENT journal. For as long as I can remember it was just a part of my daily routine whether I wanted it to be at times or not. Basically, when the inner voice inside my head tells me to write, I write.

Having the ability to look back a few years to see how much you've changed over time can truly be a game changer when it comes down to understanding why you are the way you are.

As we grow and develop in life, our perspectives change pretty significantly. If you really want to learn about yourself, I highly suggest you keep a journal and don't spare any details… your future self will thank you for it.

THIS JOURNAL BELONGS TO:

Lucy

TIMEFRAME:

MAY 2013 - SEPTEMBER 2013

Entry #1

FRIDAY MAY 31ST 2013

IT WAS AROUND NINE AND MOM WAS JUST GETTING HOME FROM WORK. Usually, she makes an entrance, but tonight she just walked right in and didn't even say hello, just asked I give her and Dad some privacy. I was a little sketched out, but I gave them their space.

About twenty or so minutes later they came up to my room and told me they had to talk to me about something. I kept quiet hoping it wasn't my eviction notice.

Dad lost his job due to new management and budget cuts and Mom was given an opportunity at work she couldn't pass up.

She's in the mortgage business, she helps people buy houses. Her new position would allow her to be the branch manager with a full house of employees under her wing.

But the job is in Charleston, South Carolina.

Yup, the fucking South.

She said the market down there is busy and she has to chase the opportunity. Also, they already bought a house, and we have to be out of this one by Wednesday.

I was speechless.

As much as I wanted to scream, I couldn't get any words out.

WHERE WOULD I LIVE? WHAT WOULD I DO? ON SUCH SHORT NOTICE? WHAT THE ACTUAL FUCK.

None of it seemed fair, until she told me there was space for me IF I wanted to move down with them.

Coulda led with that…

Dad chimed in and mentioned he had some job interviews lined up, which made me wonder how long they've been planning this for…

And why are they only just telling me now? Four days before we have to be out??

As they both glorified all that awaits them in the South, there I was fighting in my head trying to figure out what the fuck I was going to do.

I acknowledge they didn't completely abandon me because they offered me a place to stay. But. How was I going to decide where to live?

Who knew as you got older, you'd sometimes miss having things decided for you.

Mom said she didn't have a choice in the location, but thought change could be good, so she expressed interest in the position.

Her company is also paying for the moving expenses, which is also why it was happening so quickly. Apparently, I missed out on the planning because now is the time for action.

I told them I needed to think about it, so we called it a night.

Moms worked hard her entire life, I'm excited that she's making her dreams come true. I'm proud of her. I just wish we didn't have to leave our home. After all, this was the first house they bought together, it's where they brought me home from the hospital... I've spent my entire life in this house; that and this town are all I know.

Like, EVERYTHING has happened here.

I needed to clear my head; the thoughts kept pouring in and I was catching on to every single one.

I rolled a joint and climbed out onto the roof. I'm so heartbroken over this… Even the view of the stars couldn't keep me grounded tonight.

■■■

I don't want to leave. This has been my home for twenty-four years; it's literally all I know…

Which is why I think I need to go.

It's taken me awhile to find peace. And now that I have it, I don't want to do anything to harm it. I also don't want to miss out on another moment life has to offer. Change is scary, but necessary. And I think I'm due some fresh air in my life.

Not to mention a second chance at a first impression is one hell of a gift I really shouldn't let go to waste. I've learned from the mistakes I've made here, so now I know how not to screw things up when we move down there.

I don't want to be the girl who hides behind her past anymore.

I can move and finally become exactly who I've always wanted to be.

I finally managed to pause the thoughts and completely silenced my mind.

I took a deep breath in, held it, and let it out.

Tears immediately flew down my cheeks.

I had made my decision.

I would be stupid not to take this opportunity. Besides family and friends, there really isn't much going on for me here... And I know they'll still be there for me regardless of where I live.

Of course, then I wondered about how I was going to break the news to everyone. I mean I haven't even figured out what MY next steps were, so how could I know what to tell everyone else?

Here I am having a people pleasing moment. I should be focused on myself but instead I'm worried about everyone else. (You should work on this more).

I texted Scarlett and told her to swing by after work so we could catch up.

She's off for the summer semester, so she's taking extra shifts at work to save up some cash for the fall.

She was an hour and a half out, so I had some time to get my shit together.

I had the munchies, was feeling like a chicken quesadilla would do it for me, so I whipped one up.

Mom heard; she came downstairs to check on me. We talked and she put my mind at ease. She firmly believes this move will be a life-changing opportunity for all of us. I was so drawn in by her excitement, I started to believe her.

She headed back upstairs, and I did some searching around the area we're moving to.

Looked nice, I guess.

Scarlett got off work early, I told her to come in and meet me on the roof.

We talked about her day and some asshole at work, typical bullshit.

When she asked me how I was doing, I told her everything.

She thought she could get away with telling me she was happy for me, but I knew she was just as sad as I was. We've known each other for eighteen years; we grew up doing everything together. We had plans for the future.

She told me that I was making a great decision and that I owe it to myself to be selfish for once. That I was strong and would be stupid not to take the offer to move with the parents.

Both in tears, we hugged and fantasized about our new paths. For the first time in almost two decades, we were planning a future separate from each other.

Is it bad to admit that I'm a little excited to not have to live in her spotlight anymore?

Entry # 2

SATURDAY JUNE 1ST 2013

I ROLLED OUT OF BED AROUND TEN; I WAS ANXIOUS TO GET A HEAD START ON packing up my life now that I'm excited about it.

The parents weren't home, so I packed a bowl and got to work. I found some things I never thought I would see again, which probably set the tone for how the rest of the packing was going to go.

The movers will be here in three days and I'm 100% not ready for this.

I thought if I started with my closet I could conquer it quickly, but I was wrong.

Almost two hours later I had three piles of clothes that I was deciding between. After all, I was practically fantasizing on how I wanted to dress as the new me.

Though, I'm still not sure what that's going to look like yet…

If this move doesn't work out, at least I was able to cleanse and get rid of shit I no longer needed.

I spent the rest of the afternoon going through everything else I own and ended up with two boxes of stuff to donate.

I've been looking for things to spend the settlement money on, so I'm thinking a new wardrobe is the perfect place to start.

Shit. I can't believe it's been almost a year since the car accident has settled and I haven't spent a dime…

•••

Mom and Dad were in the dining room surrounded by a shit ton of paperwork and a bottle of wine. Talking about the new house, this house and everything in between…Which made me realize that I had no idea what our new home was going to look like.

They gave me the address and I pulled up the listing. The house we live in now is great, but hot damn this new place is huge!

Five bedrooms, four bathrooms, and it's 3,400sqft. I don't know what they plan to do with all that space, but I'm super excited to come home to that every day.

Turns out it's so huge because there's a mother-in-law suite attached; it's 1,000sqft and holds two bedrooms and two bathrooms. The master bathroom has a jacuzzi tub and a stand-up shower. Even the closet is huge; double what I have now!

Oh, and the main house is gorgeous… there's a deck outside large enough for hosting parties, and an in-ground pool big enough for at least a dozen people. Apparently, the housing market is cheaper in the South…

The kicker was when they told me the MIL suite was for me! While I was hoping they were going to say that I didn't want to assume and be disappointed. Their only request was that once I got established with a job, I would have to start paying rent, but that was fair, so I happily accepted.

I'll have my own walls and my own front door; I can't believe this is happening to me.

I hugged them, thanked them, told them over and over how much I appreciated everything…

They were busy so I gave them their space. Scarlett called; she needed a ride to work because her car wasn't starting.

Turns out she called out of work and got everyone together for a goodbye party. It was an awesome surprise, and it was nice to share the news with everyone.

We had a great night together.

I'm hopeful it won't be the last, but if it was, this chapter could not have closed any better than it did.

Entry #3

SUNDAY JUNE 2ND 2013

WOKE UP AND MET THE PARENTS FOR SUNDAY BREAKFAST. MY AUNT IS throwing us a going away party tonight and it's not optional.

Up until then, we spent the day packing. Managed to pack up the guest room, hall closets, laundry area, living room, and dining room… Mom doesn't waste any time. Not to mention we're donating a shit ton of furniture, so that helped lighten the load.

I decided to donate most of mine as well… after all, I have my very own apartment to furnish now, so I might as well start fresh and buy all new.

Not like I don't have the money for it…

We got to my aunts, and I spent the entire night bullshitting with my cousins. Eventually when it was time to leave, we said our goodbyes, made plans to visit, then got the fuck out of there.

Parents went to bed; I stayed up to do some more packing now that I've decided on what I was doing with some things. They'll be here tomorrow to pick it all up, so I'm a bit short on time.

I don't really have much left; I just get caught up in the little things. Plus, tomorrow is our last night here and I really didn't want to spend it packing.

After the shelter swings by, all that will remain are the mattresses and box springs, bags for our flight, and the rest of our belongings the movers are bringing down for us.

Tomorrow is when reality is going to slap me in the face that we're leaving the only home I've ever known.

I called it on the packing around midnight.

I was smoking on the roof when I got a call from Benji… we haven't spoken since our breakup six months ago.

I answered the phone, he was nearby and wanted to see me. I told him he could come by.

I wanted to cry the second our eyes met.

He asked if he could hug me… I almost felt whole again wrapped in his arms. I had to pull away before I said something I wouldn't have been able to take back.

He found out I was leaving and had to see me before I left because he misses me and still wants to be with me.

I didn't know what to say… we grew up together and dated for two years, but when we broke up it was mutual. Sort of.

We talked and concluded we were better off as friends and would always be involved in the others life in some way. In no way was it an easy conversation, but it needed to happen and were both glad it did.

We loved each other deeply, but we're in two different places in life. He wants to settle down, but I'm not ready for that yet. I've already missed out on so much… I owe it to myself to make up for lost time. Unfortunately, we couldn't move past that, so we decided it was best to break up so neither one of us was being held back from what we wanted.

We decided to have one last night together, for old times' sake.

While it's nice to have sex under the stars, the roof is not very sturdy, so we took things inside and finished on my bed.

Talk about having to be VERY cautious of echoes.

I haven't had sex since we broke up, he says he hasn't either. While it felt amazing physically, mentally I wanted to feel some type of attachment towards him again.

Having sex with him reminded me of the little moments that would take place before and after, and that's what was starting to get to me. I had no choice but to push those feelings away; for good.

He stayed the night and we fell asleep in each other's arms. I can't believe that was the last time he's ever going to hold me. The last time I'm going to smell his mahogany deodorant…

I guess you can say it was the perfect ending to who we were, and a new beginning to who we would become.

Entry #4

MONDAY JUNE 3RD 2013

BENJI LEFT EARLY IN THE MORNING, SOON AFTER THE PARENTS HEADED OUT. IT was an emotional goodbye, but we were ready this time. He left, I took a shower and got myself together for the day.

Around eleven or so, Scarlett called me, and we talked about Benji. She was happy that we got some closure, and sex; apparently, I needed both. Mom called to tell me she and Dad were running behind and needed me to pack up the kitchen and toss what needed to go.

I switched back to Scarlett and told her to come over, but she had some stuff to do so we hung up and switched to texting. I put on some music and went to town.

Almost two hours later I had everything packed up and all cleaned out. It was weird seeing the house so empty. All the memories started flashing back so I closed my eyes, sat for a minute, and took it all in.

I'm going to miss this place so fucking much…

The parents finally got home and helped me finish getting everything together. We are officially 100% packed and ready to go.

We ordered some pizza, and reminisced as we enjoyed our final meal together in this house. It wasn't long after we finished eating that the doorbell rang, it was the shelter volunteers here to pick everything up.

As each piece was removed from the house, I could feel my nerves and anxiety piling up; I was struggling more than I anticipated, so I went upstairs and smoked a bowl on the roof. Time stood still and before I knew it, the volunteers were driving off with practically my entire life in the back of their truck.

Granted it was furniture, clothes, and other miscellaneous replaceable items, it was still emotional; there were memories attached to everything we gave them.

I know positive changes lie ahead, and while I am keeping an open mind, I'm still a bit fucking scared if I'm being honest.

•••

Brainstormed with the parents in the kitchen once I calmed down. They seemed okay, but I could tell they were emotional themselves. I mean they have more memories here than I do... they got married and built their life here. I hope to have a marriage as strong as theirs someday.

They're cool people and I'm grateful for everything they've done and continue to do for me. I wouldn't be healthy today if it wasn't for them fighting for me when I wasn't able to fight for myself.

Considering all we had left to sit on were toilets and mattresses, we called it a night. I wasn't ready for bed just yet, so I decided to head to the park and swing on the swings one last time.

Walking through the neighborhood for what felt like the last time, was hard. My entire life was flashing before me, I couldn't help but follow along.

I walked past my old bus stops and pictured all those dreadful early mornings I spent waiting for the bus to arrive that was always late, yet right on time when I was a few minutes behind.

Anyway. When I made it to the park, it was thankfully empty.

The moon was nearly full, and the sky was covered with stars. It was the perfect night to star gaze and soaking under the moonlight made me feel like everything was going to be okay. I felt at peace.

By the time I made it home, I was so ready for bed; I haven't been sleeping well these past few nights.

As I laid down and drifted to sleep for the last time in this house, I made a promise to myself that I would do everything I could to make this pain that I'm feeling worth it. I have a lot of nice memories here, but I'm ready to make new ones.

Entry #5

WOKE UP, SHOWERED, AND WENT DOWNSTAIRS JUST AS DAD WAS WALKING IN the door with fresh bagels for breakfast. Usually we do that on Sundays, but this was a special occasion, not to mention our last real bagel for who knows how long.

I had a sausage, egg and cheese on a plain bagel, the parents had bacon, egg, and cheese. To this day we still poke fun at the fact that they hate how sausage tastes with egg and can't understand where I got the taste for it from.

We stood around the kitchen island eating, when Mom got a call that they needed to see her at the office before she left. Dad asked me if I wanted to go furniture shopping; of course, I did. I couldn't have gotten ready fast enough.

It was nice to spend some time with him, feels like we haven't in a while.

We talked about Moms new job and his upcoming interviews… he apologized for not telling me sooner about the move. Now that I've calmed down, I understand why they did what they did.

Growing up I was never really involved in or knew about any issues. They let me be a kid, and I will forever be grateful for that.

Thankfully Dad has already seen the place, so he knows what kind of space I have to work with. Turns out when they went away for the weekend a few months back, it was to look at houses. I mean I had the house to myself, so I didn't care to ask any questions.

He took me to a furniture outlet store, and it was practically a mini mall, there were so many options.

After about an hour, I managed to find a complete bedroom set, a small dining room table with chairs, a couch, a coffee table with matching end tables, and some lamps to scatter around the place.

Everything cost about $4,500 including delivery, so I made one hell of a good decision. They have warehouses throughout the country and can have my stuff delivered to the new house on Wednesday, right around the same time the rest of our things will be delivered.

Oh, I found a decent office desk; it has plenty of room for my computer and stationery. It even came with a chair, for only just $200. I was able to take it with me, instead of having it shipped.

Mom called. Her office threw her a surprise going away party… she was so emotional about it. She's been with the same company since she was in her early twenties. Granted she'll still be working with them, a new office in a new state is a big change.

She wasn't going to be home for a bit, so Dad and I stopped at our favorite pizzeria to enjoy the food one last time. Yes, even though we just had pizza yesterday.

I'm glad we went… I'll miss it so much. I had my first date there and it was always the go to hang out spot with everyone after school. I haven't thought about it in forever, but that's how I met Benji. Some say that if we didn't break up, we could have been a great love story.

Dad and I finished up lunch and headed out. Benji's parents have been taking more time off lately to spend together, so they have a manager now to help run things while they're away. Unfortunately, they won't be back before we leave, but they're always a phone call away.

Maybe ten minutes after Mom got home, the movers showed up. There was the dreaded knock on the door for them to come and take away all our things. While I'm trying to be positive, it still fucking hurts.

They hauled away what little furniture we had left before they broke into teams to empty out the rooms. While they were respectful, they carried our things like none of it meant anything. Everything we own is just something in a box at this point.

While I was prepared and knew this would happen, I wasn't ready for how it was going to actually make me feel. I thought I sorted my feelings out already, but things don't always go the way you planned.

I stood by my window with only my suitcase, as I watched the movers drive away with what's left of my childhood. I held in tears for as long as I could, then escaped to the roof and fucking cried.

I felt like my life was disappearing before my eyes. The house was empty, Mom was starting a new phase in her career, Dad was getting a fresh start to his, and I was going to have my own space.

But then what?

They've had time to prepare for this move, I haven't. They have an idea of what to expect when we get down there, I don't. I'm really trying to be positive about this and trust them when they say that everything will be okay.

Once I calmed down, I went back inside and found the parents in the living room. It was just down to the three of us and this empty house.

It was time to leave.

We did one final walk through together, and then we left. Just like any other day, we locked the door behind us, and we drove away; only this time we were never coming back.

They dropped me off at Scarlett's and will be back at five in the morning to come and get me. I was silent getting out of the car. They stayed the night at my aunt's.

Scarlett was hanging out in the living room when I got there.

We smoked a lot of weed and were definitely in need of some food. We were rummaging through the kitchen when her brother came downstairs. We chatted for a second, turns out he has a friend where I'm moving to who can sell me weed; I was relieved to have a safe hookup lined up.

See, things are looking up already.

Apparently, they play video games together. Her brother had to pee, so he handed me his mic and I talked to his friend for a minute. His name is Hunter and he sounded really hot; I loved the accent. He gave me his deets and that was that, kept it strictly professional.

So can't wait to meet him in person.

We finally decided and had Chinese delivered. We talked for what felt like hours about the past, the present, the future, and everything in between. We even planned a trip for her to come down and visit the week of 4th of July.

Her parents came home and sat outside with us for a few minutes before they went to bed. Her Mom cried as she hugged me goodbye.

She too was happy that I was doing something for myself after all that's happened, and she told me she wished she had done something like this when she had the chance.

I wasn't as close with Scarlett's dad because he worked a lot, but it was still an emotional goodbye and he told me to always call him if I ever needed anything. It was unexpected, but very sweet. It hadn't crossed my mind until now how much I would miss her parents… I mean I practically grew up around them.

It wasn't long after they called it a night that we did. Tomorrow is going to be a long day and I need rest.

Entry # 6

IT WAS FIVE ON THE DOT WHEN THE PARENTS ARRIVED TO PICK ME UP. I HAD only a few minutes to say goodbye to the person that is practically a sister to me.

We cried and promised to still be friends and that we'd always have each other no matter what.

She tried to make me laugh but it didn't work this time; and at that moment I knew that it was possible we may never see each other again. I got in the car, and we headed to the airport.

My mind shifted to autopilot, and I dozed off on the plane. Next thing I knew we had landed.

We had a cab take us to the new house to meet with the real estate agent for the keys. While they were all talking, I went over to my side of the house and looked around. My bedroom has french doors and right outside is a small balcony. I even have a walk-in closet with built in shelves… I made my way back to the kitchen when I heard this loud ass honking.

It was the movers and the furniture delivery drivers- they showed up at the exact same time. It was perfect. Within two hours everything was unloaded and ready to be put away.

To my surprise all my furniture was already set up; I had forgotten that I paid for them to deliver AND install. I was so excited, I had to get my bedroom done first…

Within an hour I managed to completely unpack my room- after all I did get rid of a lot of things back home, so there really wasn't a whole lot left to put away.

It felt nice when I stepped back and looked at everything. I felt like I was purified of my past or something… New environment, new house, new furniture… it was a nice feeling.

Was definitely feeling the warm and fuzzies.

While all the new furniture filled up the space, I was in desperate need to fill my closet. I was finishing up my office when Mom called asking if I wanted to have dinner with them.

Well of course I did, I didn't have any groceries yet and that's a thing for me to worry about now. It's going to be weird having dinner on my own, but I think I'll get used to it quickly.

I'm sure we'll still have dinner together some nights, but I'm looking forward to venturing out on my own.

Completely clueless to what's around, we settled on a bar around the corner. It was the closest thing we could find, and we were starving.

DUDE.

Our waiter was hot, I had to focus and make sure I wasn't staring. I mean, damn, they don't make boys like him back home.

Wish I paid attention to his name.

I was smitten. He had soft green eyes; short brown hair and he was tall. He had really nice arms, too.

I bet if I stood next to him, he would tower over me…

Suddenly the South didn't seem all that bad and I can 100% guarantee it was because of the waiter. Northern guys are cool, but Southern guys are a whole new species I look forward to exploring.

As exhausted as we all were after dinner, we headed to the store for light groceries, so we had something to get us through the night.

Buying my own groceries was… empowering. The parents offered to get mine, but I was happy to do it on my own.

Side note. People here wave… like a lot. Even to strangers?

On the way home I texted Scarlett about the waiter, but more importantly sent her pictures of all the unpacking I had done already.

I loved showing off my new space, it was so exciting.

We got home and parted ways. I mean were still attached to the same roof, but we have our own walls between us now… and I fucking love it.

I still can't believe they're allowing me to stay here.

I unpacked the groceries and plopped right into bed. I really needed to shower but I was too tired. I got my ass up, brushed my teeth, laid back in bed, and passed the fuck out.

Entry #7

THURSDAY JUNE 6ᵀᴴ 2013

I SLEPT IN TILL ABOUT ELEVEN, IT WAS AMAZING. WAKING UP IN MY OWN PLACE without my parents right around the hall is a whole new level of freedom I'm thrilled to experience.

I don't have a coffee pot yet, so I hung out in bed and fantasized about how I wanted my new life here to be.

I took a shower in my new walk-in shower that's big enough for two and it was as awesome as you'd expect.

As I was finishing up my hair, Mom texted me inviting me to go shopping with her while Dad unpacked.

Couldn't type yes fast enough.

I met her outside and we headed to the mall. I had a few rooms to fill, so we definitely shopped till we dropped.

While it's nice to spend money, I do need to be careful, so I don't run out… I need to find a job.

We stopped and grabbed some sandwiches for lunch. While we were waiting for the food to come out, Mom asked me what my plans were now that we're here and settling in.

I want to work, but I'm not exactly sure what I want to do… I just know what I don't want to do, and I refuse to move backwards. I feel like it's time to do something a little more serious.

She chimed in and asked if I was still interested in hearing about what she does for work. Of course I was. I don't know what she makes, but it's obviously good and if I can make money like her someday, I want in as soon as possible.

I want to be able to take care of myself and do the things I want, but also do something meaningful with my time.

Retail was fun, don't get me wrong, but it took a lot out on my body, and my health suffered because of it. But that's in the past and I didn't want any of that to follow me here, remember?

She gave me ALL the details… even warned me that it's a very stressful environment and it's not for everyone, but if you're passionate about it, you'll go far.

After hearing more about what she does, I told her I was serious about wanting to learn whatever she was willing to teach me. She told me if after two weeks of job shadowing, I was still interested, she would teach me everything she knew and that I would have a job if I wanted.

She told me to enjoy the summer and to get to know the area so she had time to learn her new role, and I could come sit in this Fall when it's slower.

We headed out with so much stuff; we could barely carry it all to the car. We took a different way home and the view was incredible. We drove over a river and the sunshine beating down on the water made it glimmer. We're much closer to the water here than we were back home and it's kind of nice. I don't know why I was hating on this so much; now that we're here I kind of like where we ended up.

We pulled up to the house and went our separate ways.

I threw on some music and unpacked all the things I had just bought. Two hours later and I was done… there was nothing left to buy, nothing left to clean or unpack, and all the garbage was taken out. I took some new pictures, and I sent them to Benji first; I wanted him to know that I was doing okay and that I was safe. He was sweet, he said he was happy for me.

For a second, I imagined what this tiny place would be like if it were ours…. But then I remembered why we split up in the first place and bounced back to reality.

Scarlett video chatted with me after she got off work so I could give her the grand tour. She loves it.

I made a frozen pizza for dinner and spent the night researching the area.

Entry #8

Friday June 7th 2013

I WOKE UP AROUND NINE TODAY. MADE SOME BREAKFAST AND SCROLLED AWAY on social media. It seemed I was the only one without any summer plans.

I mean, I guess moving to a new state across the country <u>could</u> count as something.

Mom texted me asking if I had any plans, they needed some help unpacking. I finished up breakfast and went over to help. It was nice to see some old stuff from back home. Family photos and old knick-knacks.

Took about two hours but everything is now unpacked, and all the garbage is out of the house. With the new furniture and all the boxes unpacked, their house looks NICE. Wi-Fi is finally set up too…

I gave them a quick tour of my place next, and they loved it.

I'm getting more excited for this new chapter.

•••

Okay, so. I was able to get some weed from Hunter. Mom is letting me borrow her car until Monday.

Get this.

HES THE WAITER FROM THE BAR.

Can you believe that? Neither one of us had any idea, until I walked in the door, and we instantly recognized each other.

Oh, and he lives right down the block, like a few houses down…

Now that the dots had been connected, I was nervous he was going to pick up on how attracted I was to him.

He broke the ice by offering to pack a bowl, on him, he said he lets people sample when they first buy.

He handed me the green hit and next thing I knew, I was stoned. His stuff was good, it was strong, and I was totally feeling it.

I think he knew I was too, he asked me if I was okay. I told him I was, and I tried to play it cool- key word there is tried.

I was high so my mind was everywhere, thankfully he led the conversation. He asked me how I met Scarlett, and where I ended up moving to. Maybe I was just high, but I swear I saw a smirk when I mentioned I was the one who just moved in down the street.

I asked him about the area, and he gave me the inside scoop; basically, it's a quiet neighborhood and people mostly keep to themselves. I thought he was joking with me at first, but he told me about this abandoned treehouse and how I should check it out sometime. He sarcastically added I could bring my boyfriend there when he comes to visit me.

I was maybe a little too quick to respond when I told him there is no boyfriend…

"That's cool". That was literally his response.

I was like, "Totally".

I felt awkward so I brought our conversation back to business, paid for the weed, and went on my way.

He looks really hot when he games by the way. His whole look had me feeling some type of way, and he was only wearing a fucking T-shirt and shorts. It's the arms, definitely the arms.

I pulled up to the house and remembered I needed some groceries, so I dropped my stuff off in the house and ran to the store. I called Scarlett on my way and told her all about what just happened.

She tried to convince me that I should pursue him, but a guy isn't what I need in my life right now. Of course, a summer romance in a new state sounds sexy, but he's also my weed guy, not to mention my <u>only</u> weed connection here, and that is not something I want to mess with.

I finally got her to change the topic. We talked about how cool it is to not be living with parents, at least under the same roof anymore. She was jealous so I told her she would be able to enjoy it when she comes down to visit.

For dinner tonight, I decided to try out a new pizza place. I ordered from a place around the corner that had pretty good reviews. Though I heard the food tasted different down here so I wasn't sure what to expect.

While I waited for the food to be delivered, I packed a bowl, filled the tub with hot soapy water, and sunk right in. I lit some candles, watched a show on my phone and felt calm for the first time in a while.

When we moved here, I promised myself I would move on and let go of the past. And that's exactly what I'm going to do.

I finished up not long before the pizza came, it was good, I'll order from them again. I cozied up on the couch and fell asleep to some tv show playing.

Entry # 9

THE VIEW FROM THE BALCONY IS INCREDIBLE. IT OVERLOOKS THE BACKYARD SO I can chill out there without anyone seeing me. There's vacant land behind the house, so there are no neighbors to deal with, just trees.

With coffee in one hand and a joint in the other, I stood in the doorway as the morning breeze brushed against my naked body.

I've always wanted to try that.

Hunter texted me, he wanted to check in and see how the weed was treating me.

Me: "Of course you would text me while I was smoking. The weeds great, thanks!".

Hunter: "I guess it's one of my superpowers. I'm glad the weed makes you feel good."

I said, "Thanks. So, tell me more about these superpowers of yours."

I went on with my day and found a patio furniture store.

I headed over and walked around until I spotted this super cute bistro set. I had to have it; it was perfect. It was a light purple color, and the chairs were super comfortable.

I made my way home and set everything up, it looked amazing, I was so excited.

I headed to the kitchen and made some lunch so I could enjoy my first meal outside; I made a sandwich.

A few minutes after I sat down to eat, Hunter texted me back: "Sorry for the delay, it got a little crazy over here. I could show you better than I could tell you."

I wasn't sure how to respond, so I took my time in getting back to him.

I looked around to see if there were any used car lots and ended up finding a few with some I liked. I talked to Dad and he's going to take me tomorrow so we can look… fingers crossed I find something. I don't need or want anything fancy, I just need it to run, so a cheap jalopy will do; my budget is five thousand and under.

I got a little hot, so I went inside and watched some tv for a bit. The humidity here sucks.

I totally drifted because it was dinner time, and I had no idea what to make. Having to plan meals and fend for myself is not something I'm used to, so I really need to get a grip and figure it out. Considering all the meat was frozen and I had nothing defrosted, I settled on simple sauce and pasta.

As I was sitting down to eat, I realized I didn't text Hunter back.

I said: "That sounds like trouble, but I'll take you up on that".

You don't need a guy right now, Lucy, you need friends…

He replied quickly: "Cool, let's meet at the treehouse I was telling you about, I promise it's safe. By the time I get home from work it'll be close to eleven, is that too late?"

I told him that was fine, he sent me the address and it was only a ten-minute walk.

I was nervous as hell… we were flirting hard, and I totally (and out of character) went along with it.

I forgot how dangerous flirting could be…

I thought about calling Scarlett, but I'd rather just tell her about it tomorrow instead.

I rummaged through my closet to find something cute but appropriate for the situation and landed on some cute jeans and a T-shirt.

I was nervous but excited. I wasn't sure what to expect. Benji was the last guy I've been with, really the only guy I've been with.

I reminded myself that there's nothing to be nervous about. I'm looking for a friend, nothing more… I just need to chill on the flirting.

I got there before he did.

The treehouse had two swings built off the side, and only a single night light to see with. It was old, but it looked intact. I swung on the swings until he showed up.

He wore jeans and a T-shirt. He had a hat on. He looked <u>good</u>. He also smelled like food, fried food.

He sat on the swing next to me and we passed a joint back and forth until I called it quits, his weed is so strong, yo.

We exchanged conversation and talked about our days; avoiding the very reason that brought us here.

I finally asked him what was so special about this treehouse, so we ditched the swings and climbed inside.

You could tell that people come and go, there were blankets and empty alcohol bottles lying around.

He cleared the floor for us and told me to lie down next to him and to look up. I followed his direction and when I looked up, I saw the most incredible night sky I had ever seen.

I started to laugh, and I was like, "How did you know this was my favorite thing to do". He replied, "It's one of my superpowers".

Fuck meeee, I was smitten.

There weren't as many lights around us, so we were able to see the sky more clearly.

It never looked this good back home…

He asked me how I was handling the move. I told him we were skipping a few steps, but he insisted and reminded me that we're technically long-time friends because we're friends of friends. He's cute, so I didn't argue.

I told him I had a choice on whether I wanted to come down here or not and how I was against it at first.

I also told him I got out of a serious relationship six months ago and was looking forward to a fresh start. I was rambling and added that while I was attracted to him, I needed to be clear about only wanting to be friends right now. Then I told him I realized I was flirting with him earlier and needed to apologize for giving him the wrong impression.

He looked at me in silence with this grin on his face. It made me nervous, so I told him he had to spill his secrets now that he knew mine…

He confessed that he already knew who I was when I came into his bar because Scarlett's brother had sent him a picture of me.

Was hyper focused on wanting to know what picture was sent…

He told me he had gotten out of a serious relationship himself about eight months ago, so he wasn't looking for anything either. He then added that we could be friends and still have fun… but only if I was up for it.

I'm pretty sure I knew what he was proposing but I'm a bit naïve in this department, so I told him I was serious.

He said he was too.

I told him we barely knew each other... He said that only gave us plenty of things to talk about.

He pulled out the rest of the joint and we puffed it back and forth. We changed the subject, and I showed him a picture of my purple table.

He teased me about buying a purple table.

A little while had passed, I was starting to feel sleepy, so I called it a night.

He asked me if he could walk me home and so to do the opposite of what I would normally do which is to make some silly excuse to say no, I told him yes.

Ten minutes felt like fifteen minutes… The sexual tension was killing me and all we were doing was walking. It's the way he carries himself; so strong and confident. I want a taste of it.

I need to refocus; I promised myself I would make this move worth it.

But wouldn't I be doing the exact opposite by not exploring things with Hunter? After all, he made it very clear himself he doesn't want a relationship, so….

Where's the harm in having a little fun? If we're both on the same page from the start, feelings can't get hurt.

Entry #10

SUNDAY JUNE 9TH 2013

I WOKE UP AROUND NINE AND LAID IN BED FOR A BIT UNTIL I MADE SOME COFFEE and sat outside.

I love this balcony by the way, it's amazing.

Dad and I weren't looking at cars until one, so I had some time to chill.

I thought more about last night… I had to tell Scarlett. Or did I? Maybe it was time to stop running to her all the time.

We have a great friendship, but it's not always the best sometimes. Though since this guy is her brother's friend and they clearly talk, I should probably tell her what happened.

I called and gave her the details.

She said I totally friend zoned him, but that's what I wanted. Right?

…

About two hours into looking, I finally walked out with the keys to my very own car! I bought a used 2010 Chevy Camaro; has some miles on it but it's in great shape.

I picked a place on the map that didn't seem too far out of reach… about a two-and-a-half-hour drive. I had the windows down and the music up… it was amazing. I landed myself at this park with hidden waterfalls that were highly recommended by strangers on the internet.

It was a cute spot; I almost said little but there was actually a lot in the area. Small shops and restaurants covered the streets like blankets. Bakeries, bookstores, art galleries, lunch spots, coffee shops; you name it, they had one.

There was even an ice-skating rink! It was closed of course because it's like a hundred fucking degrees out, but it was cool to see. Ice skating is the best; it reminds me of home.

I made my way around and found the waterfalls that everyone had raved about, totally worth the drive.

It was about to be dark soon, and while I knew the streetlights would protect me, I was still in an unfamiliar area. I walked along the bridge and took in the view of the sunset poking through the waterfalls.

It was incredible.

You know who would love this? Benji.

I know we've been apart for a while and I know that I was the one who broke things off, but that doesn't mean it still doesn't hurt sometimes. While I don't hurt as much as I did in the beginning, I still miss him every now and then. He's always been a huge part of my life.

It was about nine when I finally checked the time, didn't realize I had been exploring for that long. Shops started to close and there were less people out walking than before, I decided on a place to eat so I could head home.

It's nice not having to get up early tomorrow and since I have my own car now, it doesn't matter when I get home. Ugh, life is pretty fucking amazing right now. My heart may still hurt a little, but my soul is finally seeing the light again.

For the first time in a really long time, I feel free.

I found a hole in the wall sandwich shop and couldn't resist trying it out. They even had coffee which came in handy for the almost three-hour drive back home.

I checked out the menu and I saw all my favorites, but I was kind of thinking I should try something new. I asked the waitress what she recommended and after asking me my favorite flavors, she suggested a Cuban sandwich. It tasted amazing and is now my new favorite.

I crushed it, along with a cup of coffee, so I was ready to hit the road.

The drive back was nice, and it was cool not having to rush.

I got home a little after twelve which wasn't too bad.

I still can't believe I have my own car… Things are so different now and we haven't even been here a full week yet.

Entry # 11

I WOKE UP AROUND NINE BUT STAYED IN BED FOR A BIT. WAS A LITTLE SORE from all the exploring so I wasn't in any rush.

Once I did get up and moving, I went to the auto parts store and bought some supplies; got a steering wheel cover, cell phone holder, some cleaning and emergency supplies.

It was raining outside, so I went back home and read for a bit, ate some lunch. I lost track of time. When I checked my phone, I had two missed calls from Dad- oops. I ran over and they were just sitting down to eat so I didn't miss much.

We did our thing, checked in with each other and went our separate ways after we cleaned up.

The rain stopped and it felt amazing outside, I sat out on the balcony and smoked a little; thought about how I wanted to spend my summer. Most importantly, I needed to figure out how to make some friends.

I'll admit, I'm not always the best at that; I know I can be a little guarded sometimes, so I really need to open up a little more and relax. This is a new beginning after all, and I don't want to fuck it up. Things are going way better than expected, I want to keep the fun going for as long as I can.

From here on out I will be more open to trying new things and exploring new opportunities.

While I'm going to work on myself, I also want to enjoy the summer. That's what I'm here to do anyway, right? I didn't make this sudden abrupt move to do the same old shit I did back home…

Entry #12

TUESDAY JUNE 11TH 2013

NOW THAT I'VE GOT A PLACE TO CALL MY OWN, AND MY OWN CAR, I REALLY need to put in some work on the wardrobe a little bit. I just think it's time for a change.

After all, I have lost some weight and it would be nice to have some clothes that fit well… I made a coffee to go, and I hit up the mall.

Before I could bring myself to get out of the car and into a store, I paused because I wasn't really sure what I was shopping for; I guess I wasn't sure who I wanted to be. There are still parts of me I don't particularly love, but I think now is the time to finally move on and let those insecurities go.

At least I'm going to try.

I told myself I would try on whatever I wanted, regardless of what it was. I want to be able to wear what I want to wear, no longer what I have to settle with. One store was too big, the other too small… shopping sucked.

Now that I've toned up some, it'll hopefully be a little easier. I still managed to keep my thick shape, but now I'm more evened out. I worked my ass off to get here so now it's time to enjoy it.

I got new jeans, shorts, some really cute shirts, sneakers, wedges, summer hoodies… and believe it or not, I bought some new bras and underwear.

It's nice stuff, like expensive sexy stuff. It actually fits and most importantly, I bought it for me instead of some guy I was wanting to impress.

Stuffing my trunk with new clothes and shoes was liberating… I sat for a few minutes to soak it all in before driving home.

My life is mine again, I deserve this.

I teared up for a minute, then headed home to fill up my closet. About 75% of my old clothes were gone.

Too big? Gone. Too loose? Gone. Small holes? Garbage. Faded? Garbage.

It was very nice. Now granted I don't have anywhere specific to wear these clothes to yet, I am now prepared for when I do.

Also having all your shoes lined up together in your closet is fucking amazing and I absolutely love it.

I got a random text message from Hunter. He saw me with all my bags and asked me if I had just robbed a mall- I forgot he lived down the street, he must have driven by when I was walking inside. I told him I went shopping for a new wardrobe and he said I should send him some pictures of what I got.

I didn't reply.

Instead, I packed a bowl, took a few hits, and I tried everything on again now that I was home and in my comfort zone.

I thought more about Hunter.

I mean, I just sent this guy that is clearly into me as much as I may be into him, to the friendzone, in a pretty romantic treehouse. I don't want a relationship, and neither does he. We both admitted that. I do also know that I'm ready to get back out in the world.

Benji was really the only guy I've dated and been with, so it would be fun to see what else is out there. I'm not saying I need to be in a relationship to be happy, but I do need some excitement to keep me on my toes. If Hunter just so happens to cross paths, who am I to stop him?

I threw on a new bra, a button-down shirt, and a necklace. I left the top two buttons open, and I snapped a few pictures until I got a tasteful looking one.

Along with the picture I said, "I think you were on to something the other night. What do you think of my new necklace?

You could see very little bra, but definitely some top boob.

He started typing almost immediately. I was high so I was a little paranoid… it was the first "tasteful" picture I've taken since the weight loss.

Hunter: "How do you mean? I think it looks great! Do you need any help taking it off?"

Me: "So you're going to make me spell it out for you, huh? That would be great, it was actually a challenge to put on."

Hunter: "You didn't think I was going to make it easy for you, did you? After all, you did friend zone me hard, and in the sacred romantic treehouse of all places."

Me: "Damn, well I didn't know it was sacred. I guess I do owe you one then... The other night you mentioned that it was okay to be friends and still have fun... What did you mean by that? Exactly."

Hunter: "Why don't I come over after work tonight so we can talk."

Me: "That sounds good."

Hunter: "You good to hang around for a bit? I get off in about two hours."

Me: "I know you're busy. Just come on in when you get here, doors unlocked."

I threw in a frozen dinner, showered, and munched on it while I dried my hair, threw on some light makeup, and put on the same look I was wearing in the picture. Only this time I wore these new silky sweatpants I just bought instead of the jean shorts.

I lit a different scented candle in every room confusing the fuck out of my nose and spent the rest of the time on the couch trying to calm my nerves.

Who is this confident badass I've suddenly become? And where has she been all my life?

Around nine thirty he texted me he was heading this way. Thankfully I had been smoking a hybrid strain all day, so I was fairly mellow for the most part.

Just as I was packing a fresh bowl, he walked in the door. We made instant eye contact.

He too was wearing good ole sweatpants, a band T-shirt and of course, the signature hat. No doubt he looked hot, cozy hot.

He sat down on the opposite end of the couch leaving some space in between us.

I handed him the bowl, he took a few hits and talked about his day. He asked me about mine and you know, we just moved right along with the small talk.

I had a cooking show on in the background, apparently, he likes to cook. He told me he wants to cook for me sometime and when I asked if he was any good, he said he could show me better than he could tell me.

I told him I was going to hold him to it.

He said he hopes I do.

He flashed me a smile and my brain melted.

We eventually reached a brief moment of silence.

I stood up and asked him if he wanted anything to drink.

My heart was racing, and I think it was loud enough for him to hear it.

I grabbed us some water, and he met me halfway. When I had turned around, he grabbed my waist and pulled me in close to his.

He lifted my chin up until our eyes met. He asked me if I was sure I wanted this.

I was so nervous, I'm not entirely sure if I blinked or not.

I said yes.

He leaned in for a kiss, I dropped the water bottles.

He took complete control. Even my fantasies couldn't have prepared me for what he's got me thinking he's going to do to me.

He asked if he could taste me.

Ugh, fuck yeah ya can.

I nodded yes.

Thank God I got waxed before we moved.

I was just down to my bra; the rest of my clothes were off. He had his shirt off, but his pants were on.

He turned his hat backwards. I almost creamed just from that.

He pretty much made out with my clit. There's no other way to describe it. I couldn't keep quiet very well, he caught on to what made me tick and he used it against me. He was communicating with my body, and I've never experienced that kind of sex before.

I was so hot for him. He made me feel really good.

He could tell that I was on the edge; he told me to wait because he wasn't done with me yet.

I enjoyed the ride and held on for as long as I could.

He stopped and told me he wanted to change positions so he could finish me off.

We moved to my room. He took his hat off and got situated on the bed.

He told me to sit on his face.

I hesitated.

He said, "Trust me".

I did what he told me to do and sure enough, he buried his face into my pussy.

I reached back so I could finally get a feel for what he had going on and no surprise he was on the larger side. I couldn't hold it in any longer, I finally came. On his face.

We had the "all clear" speech and discussed boundaries. He did wrap up, though I considered telling him he didn't have to.

I think he likes how vocal I am, the louder I get the tighter he grabs me.

We finished with my legs over his shoulders. Watching was better than I expected it to be.

I excused myself to freshen up, he did the same. Then we hydrated and smoked a bowl in the kitchen.

It was a little after twelve. We fooled around for almost two fucking hours.

He's coming back again tonight at seven thirty to prove those cooking skills he was raving about. He's bringing the food and I'm grabbing the alcohol.

I walked him out and we said goodnight.

I don't have a fucking clue on how I am going to handle this.

How is he so perfect? There's gotta be a catch. I really hope there isn't one. I don't want there to be one is what I should have said.

Entry #13

WOKE UP IN DESPERATE NEED OF CAFFEINE.

Two cups later and I still didn't know what to think of last night. If we can have sex without any strings attached, then what's the fucking problem?

I got dressed and went on with my day. I had liquor to pick up, laundry to do and things to clean so that was pretty much how I spent my Wednesday.

Scarlett called me, she heard from her brother that Hunter was cooking for me tonight.

I told her I was going to call her after and tell her everything, but she wanted the inside scoop on what led to dinner.

I gave her a recap of last night. She thinks I should date him, but I really don't want to be someone's girlfriend right now.

She and I talked on the phone up until Hunter showed up. He had a few bags of groceries along with this big ass grin on his face.

While he did the prepping, I made us drinks.

He didn't mind me sitting on the counter talking with him while he did all the work. He made steak, scallops, roasted potatoes, and mixed vegetables.

My kitchen has never smelled so good… there was a mixture of butter, garlic, herbs and spices, and more garlic. Makes me want to learn how to be a better cook.

We sat down to eat, both about two drinks in at that point. Everything tasted great.

I broke the silence and told him I had fun last night.

He told me he did too.

I wasn't sure what to do next, so I got up to start cleaning, he followed me into the kitchen and refilled our drinks. He then poured us each a shot and proposed the friends with benefits idea.

I told him I would agree, but only if we made a few things clear… We had to be honest with each other, safe, and no sleepovers. We took a shot in acceptance of our new friendship terms before destroying each other's bodies.

I gave him head at the end and he finished in my mouth. Swallowing is gross, but I know he'll get me back for it, so it's worth it.

He had a lot of energy so sex pretty much sobered us up, meaning he was good to drive and go home, not too long after we called it a night. I showered and did my thing - smoked a little smoke and now here I am.

Having an attractive male friend that I can sleep with and not have to deal with otherwise, is going to be a dream. We clearly vibe well and knowing we have a person in common is kind of comforting.

I'm excited to have some fun and give this a shot.

Entry #14

THURSDAY JUNE 13TH 2013

I WOKE UP TO ABOUT A DOZEN TEXT MESSAGES FROM SCARLETT; SHE WAS dying to know how it went last night. I got myself together and called her while I made coffee, she was on her way to work.

I spilled the deets, and she was so excited for me. She expects us to break the no sleepover rule.

Won't be me.

She had to get to work, which made me realize I had nothing planned for the day.

Tell you what, how this week has gone, is not at all what I was expecting to happen.

New wardrobe, new car, new place, all new furniture AND I now have a new friend who just so happens to sell me weed and has sex with me. This move was a great decision.

I decided to go on a bike ride so I could get a feel for the area. I put on some music and didn't pay attention to anything that wasn't in front of me. Until Mom called; she invited me over for dinner.

I got lost on the way back, so thank goodness for GPS. I ended up biking ten miles.

Dad grilled some chicken; Mom made a salad and some sides. We talked over dinner and caught up on life. Thankfully we made it without either one of them asking about Hunter's jeep; I mean I'm sure they saw it.

Unless, since I'm a little more independent now, they're giving me a little more privacy than the usual questionnaire I would get from time to time. I guess I won't sweat it until I have to.

I texted Hunter a little, but not much. He slept in, gamed before work and that was that. No big aftermath conversation, surprisingly. Which made me realize this could really work since we're able to separate the two.

I spent the rest of the evening reading outside, and I smoked for a bit. Overall, pretty chill day.

Entry #15

FRIDAY JUNE 14TH 2013

I WOKE UP THIS MORNING NOT REALLY HAVING ANY PLANS FOR THE DAY. GOT some food and coffee in me, did my makeup just because. Drove my ass out to the beach; not usually my "go to" scene but it was nice to check out. The smell of the salty ocean soothed my busy mind.

I set myself up with a blanket and umbrella for cover. No bathing suit yet, but I will get there. A tank top and shorts were a big enough start; it's nice when you finally feel comfortable with your body and what you're wearing.

I dipped my toes in the water. It reminded me of the beach back home. Felt a little home sick for a moment and caught myself reminiscing on the past.

I loved the beach when I was younger, it wasn't until I got older and started feeling awkward about the way I looked that I started to steer away from going.

Looking back, I missed out on so much because I was uncomfortable with the way I looked (when I had literally no reason to be). I think if I wasn't teased so much, I wouldn't have felt the way I felt. I don't know.

Now, easier said than done because I'm in better shape, but honestly, I worked hard to get here, and I deserve to feel good about myself and be proud of the progress I've made. I beat the odds set against me and that's a pretty damn good feeling.

I am living proof that you can recover from your past.

About three hours later I decided to head out and get home, I was a little hungry, but it was kind of late for lunch, so I considered an early dinner.

I decided on chicken parmesan; I haven't had it in a while. I poured myself a glass of wine and went to town in the kitchen.

Which reminds me, I need to go food shopping.

About an hour later I was sitting down to eat; it's nice sitting at my own table.

I barely had any wine left in the bottle by the time I was done cleaning up. I checked my phone for the first time in a bit and had two missed calls from Scarlett.

She had work gossip, so I opened another bottle, and we drank together on the phone, bullshitting back and forth the whole time, it was great.

It wasn't until after we hung up that I realized how drunk I was.

I made some french fries and watched tv until I had a call coming in from Benji. I was curious, so I answered.

He told me he drove past the old house today and saw the new family that moved in, and it made him think of me.

He then asked me if I had made any friends yet and if any guys managed to swoop me up.

I told him I was still working on the friend's part and changed the subject.

He burned one on the phone with me "for old times' sake" and once he was high, he started getting chatty.

He's been thinking about our goodbye and was wondering if I had thought about it too. To be honest, I did when it happened, but I haven't thought about it since. Maybe that's because I'm having sex with Hunter, but who knows. I didn't tell him that though, obviously.

As the conversation continued, he slowed things down and lowered his voice. He told me he misses me.

He's such a smooth talker and I'm a total sucker for it when I'm drunk.

I was serious when I told him I moved on. I know it's okay to miss him, it's just, we broke up for a reason and I didn't move down here just to fall back into old habits.

I told him I missed him too and reminded him I'm always just a phone call away.

I managed to get off the phone quickly after and pretty much fell right to sleep; it was late anyway, and I had drunk a shit ton of wine. I don't know how I lasted as long as I did.

$\mathcal{E}$ntry #16

I DIDN'T SET AN ALARM LAST NIGHT, SO I WOKE UP A LITTLE CLOSE TO ONE.

Not like I had major plans or anything, I didn't intend on sleeping in so late, but I guess I needed it. Had a text from Benji that he enjoyed talking with me last night, I replied with a smiley face.

Brutal truth time, I'm not in love with him anymore. While a part of me will always love him, I've moved on. It's time to start living my life the way I want to for myself, not those around me.

I had some coffee and got my shit together to go food shopping, needed major groceries. It's a beautiful feeling being able to stock the fridge yourself.

I made a sandwich for lunch and hung out on the balcony. Dad called and let me know that the pool guy was coming by sometime in the afternoon so we could start using the pool tonight. Excited for that. Not sure how much they'll use it, but I definitely will.

I don't know why I felt the need to do this after I ate, but I decided to look for a new bathing suit.

It was harder than I thought, but that was probably because I had psyched myself out on the drive to the store.

It was a struggle, but an hour later, I ended up leaving with a two piece.

Made it home in time to be the first to enjoy a swim. Even snagged a picture of myself and damn do I look good in a two-piece pool side.

Hunter texted me. We haven't talked much since our dinner, just a little here and there on Thursday. He apologized, said work had been hectic but he wanted to check in. He's sweet.

He came over after work for a midnight swim.

He kept his boxers and his hat on, I was in my new bathing suit of course.

I caught him looking me up and down as we undressed.

We sat by the edge of the pool with our feet in the water and passed a joint back and forth. The only light we had was from the moon, so we had to pass carefully.

We were flirting hard, and it wasn't long until my legs were wrapped around his face, and he was eating me out poolside.

It was super risky, we and I mean I, had to be REALLY quiet. Parents were sleeping not too far away. It was intense.

I joined him in the pool, and our bodies intertwined. We made out like high school virgins until we eventually had enough of the fourplay and moved to my place. Though the chlorine smell poked the vibe, so we took a shower together.

Another thing to check off my nonexistent bucket list... Benji and I never showered together now that I think about it.

We washed each other's bodies and soaked up every second of every minute we were in there together.

I wasn't up for shower sex, so we moved things over to my bed and went from there. We didn't wrap it up, this time he pulled out and came on my chest. Definitely using the pull-out method moving forward… we agreed it feels so much better raw.

It'll be okay. This is what birth control was made for.

Entry #17

SUNDAY JUNE 16ᵀᴴ 2013

WE HAD OUR FIRST SUNDAY BREAKFAST SINCE MOVING. MOM WENT ALL OUT, probably one of the biggest breakfasts we've ever had. Made me wonder if something was up, but they assured me all the secrets had been spilled.

We spent the afternoon together hanging out by the pool. The parents did a little landscaping before finally jumping in.

It's mind blowing how much has changed in the little time we've been here… even they seem happier.

I went food shopping with Mom, she asked me how I was doing, and it felt great to not have to lie. I thanked her again for allowing me to move down here with them.

I mean shit, so far moving here has been one of the best decisions I've made… and the summer has only just started. I hope I'm not getting ahead of myself, but I really believe things are different now. I mean it, like I actually feel different.

We concluded our family outing with chicken wings, steak, and sides for dinner. Overall decent day.

I showered, watched a romcom in bed, got stupid high, and well, here I am.

I will admit, I am proud of myself for keeping up with this journal. I do miss writing and it would be nice if I could stay consistent with it so I can look back later and see all that's changed. Writing makes me feel good about myself, and whatever affect its having on me, is working.

Entry #18

SPENT THESE LAST TWO DAYS BY THE POOL READING, AND SWIMMING IN between chapters.

Dad's new job starts tomorrow and Mom's feeling more comfortable in hers.

I bought an elliptical so I can still work out on days I either don't want to bike or can't because of bad weather. I'm pretty excited about it. I even investigated this yoga app so I can start working on my inner peace and flexibility a little bit.

Side note. I really like where I am right now, and I want to do my best to stay here. I've made so much progress and I'm happy; happier than I've been in a while.

I wasn't feeling up to cooking anything special, so I made a grilled chicken salad for dinner.

Later once the humidity dialed down, I took a walk over to the treehouse. It was the perfect night; I could see all of the stars. Thankfully it was empty, which made me wonder if it was really a hot spot or not.

I hung out for about an hour, had some music playing in the background and just relaxed under the stars.

On my walk home, Hunter texted me that he was heading home soon and wanted to know if I wanted company. Can't have sex while I'm on my period, so I told him I was just going to hang out tonight and do my own thing.

I made some popcorn and I've got a movie playing in the background. We spent the night texting back and forth, talking about random things until he asked me if I was in bed yet so we could lay down together.

Once we were both settled in bed, there was a brief pause in his response. I then started getting a series of messages from Hunter, explaining in full detail what he wanted to do to me tonight if we were together. I was so turned on by the end of it, my stomach was in knots… and men think women don't experience our own version of blue balls…

Entry #19

FRIDAY JUNE 21ST 2013

THE 4TH OF JULY IS TWO WEEKS AWAY AND SCARLETT CAN'T MAKE IT. Truthfully, I saw that coming.

Not to mention, what the hell is there to even do around here?

I texted Hunter for the inside scoop, instead he invited me out with him and his friends. Didn't say what we were doing, but he said other girls of similar age will be there so he can introduce me to new people. Speaking of, I still don't know how old he is.

I did a little yoga and spent some time on the elliptical today, wasn't feeling a bike ride in this 90-degree weather we're having right now. Yuck.

I know I haven't written in here much this week, there's just not a whole lot going on. I'm just doing my thing and enjoying my own company. Nuff said.

Entry #20

I totally and completely jinxed myself, I was doing so well staying caught up.

The weather has been incredible, so I've been taking full advantage of the yard. Sunbathing is my new favorite thing but that could very well be my new bathing suit talking.

I noticed something today. Now that I'm not around it, I realize how toxic my friends were back home. Whatever I did always resulted in some type of joke or thing to tease me about. My anxiety has gotten a little better and I can almost guarantee that's why. Hell, no one really responds to me much more anyway; maybe it's for the best.

On a more positive note.

Flirting all day with Hunter is fun. I've been working on my nudes' game; while I don't send my face, I still try to be a little creative.

The parents are having a party tomorrow night with a bunch of people from their jobs. A little jealous of how quickly they made friends, but obviously I can't make friends in an environment I'm not in yet.

While I'm excited for them, I'll probably just pop in for some food and that will be the end of that.

Today I did some yoga and went for a bike ride around the neighborhood… it's nice to get out on the bike and explore from time to time.

I found a trail and it led me down this path surrounded by giant trees, the sunshine poked through the branches and leaves, and I came out on the other side passing over a white drawbridge. It was a scene taken straight from a fairytale; I kid you not. Charleston is beautiful, I may never go back home.

I even did a few laps around a cemetery. I know how that might sound, but there was little to no traffic and the view was incredible. The birds were chirping, the trees were full, and all the flowers were fresh… it was peaceful.

Moving here was hard, but so incredibly worth it. I'm really proud of myself for making this change.

Entry #21

FRIDAY JUNE 28ᵀᴴ 2013

OKAY, I'M JUST GOING TO FORWARD OVER TO THE JUICY STUFF. IT'S A LITTLE after midnight but I'm finally sobering up.

The party the parents hosted was fucking nuts.

Mom introduced me to all her coworkers, Dads too, but one of them stood out. He's the youngest guy at mom's job, his name is Austin and he's twenty-eight.

He's taller than me, has brown hair, brown eyes, a beard, and tattoos. Also has a cute Southern charm and likes to drink the hard stuff.

We got to talking and apparently his down time consists of racing and working on go karts.

Sexy right.

We managed to break away from the crowd and stood out front in the driveway talking. He showed me some videos of races he's been in, and we continued talking in between sipping drinks. Found out he's 420 friendly, so we moved the conversation back to my place and I packed a bowl or two for us to smoke.

We puffed a few puffs; the conversation was flowing, and we were definitely vibing.

I had to remind him that he works for my mom, but that didn't stop him from coming onto me. We were making out on the couch when he suddenly stopped.

He pulled back and told me that before we went any further, he needed to be honest with me.

He told me he's working on himself and in doing so, is choosing to be celibate.

I told him I appreciated the honesty and respected his decision.

Though I became painfully curious to know what he was like in bed, obviously I wasn't going to tell him that.

I proceeded to stand up and straighten myself up when he stopped me and said that didn't mean he couldn't still make me feel good… talk about a fucking unicorn. He completely caught me off guard.

I straddled him on the couch; he bit my ear lobes, kissed up and down my neck…

It's like he knew every single spot I wanted him to touch. It's a shame he's not having sex right now, he's obviously really fucking good at it.

We changed positions so he was now lying on top of me.

The eye contact was intense, he looked me right in the eyes and rubbed my clit with his thumb. We made out while he played with me until I came. I then excused myself to the bathroom so I could compose myself.

While I was glad it didn't go any further, did I really need another guy to fool around with? When I returned, I found him on the couch with some water and he was packing a new bowl.

I sat down with him, and we smoked. I apologized for my vocals and explained that I can get kind of loud sometimes.

He told me he took it easy on me because he didn't know what I was into. I told him he didn't need to worry about me, but he insisted he knew, so I told him.

Well, I must have talked about a similar kink because his vibe changed. I don't know what I said, but something caught his attention that he couldn't get past.

I blame the alcohol and the weed.

We made out on the couch again, but fully clothed.

The sexual tension drove me nuts; I told him we should probably stop before we took things too far.

He told me I was probably right.

I think he and I had snuck away for too long anyway, so I'm hoping nobody noticed. We agreed if anyone asked, we were talking out front and he was showing me his racing videos.

We exchanged numbers and wrapped up whatever just happened. He told me he had a lot of fun tonight and hopes to see me again, though maybe this time something a little more clothed so we could get to know each other better. I agreed, he hugged me goodnight and then he left.

I took a shower and called it a night. I did peak outside and saw there was still a decent amount of people, so I think our secret is safe.

Tonight, was totally and completely unexpected. While I can't believe it happened, I wasn't regretting it either.

As I sit here writing it all down, my mind shoots over to Hunter.

I mean technically, I did not have sex with Austin and I'm not dating Hunter, we just agreed to sleep together every now and then with no strings attached. Plus, he's a guy so he could be fucking other girls too, who knows. As long as were safe, we're straight.

I mean it's okay to have male friends, plus Austin works with Mom and I'll be looking into a job there so... I don't need any trouble in the workplace before I even get started.

Entry #22

SATURDAY JUNE 29TH 2013

WHEN I WOKE UP THIS MORNING, I HAD A TEXT FROM HUNTER AND AUSTIN.

Hunter texted me last night asking if I was free (thank God he didn't just stop by), and Austin said he had fun but hopes he didn't ruin anything by moving too fast.

I was slightly hungover from last night and in desperate need of some caffeine before I could answer either of them.

I texted Hunter first. I apologized for not responding and told him I was at the parents' party, so I wasn't by my phone much.

Which wasn't a lie.

Then I tackled Austin and told him I felt the same, though we were drinking so we get a second chance. He replied with, "So does that mean I can see you again"?

I told him, "Yes, but I have a little truth of my own I should share with you".

I told him my plans for the summer and made it clear that I wasn't looking for anything serious.

I didn't re read my response a dozen times before sending, I just typed as it came to mind and hit send. Unfiltered.

Considering he's on a similar path, he understood, and mentioned we could be each other's accountability partners if I wanted. I was down for it, seemed like a good way to keep things platonic. Plus, now I know what NOT to talk about around him. Or do I know exactly what to talk about?

I got myself somewhat together to head next door to help with some cleaning; the parents were out in the yard when I found them.

Before I could say a word Dad asked where I had "disappeared" off to last night. I told him I was out front talking to Austin. Mom made a comment that she thought we should date. I was like, "Mom, that's one of your employees". She laughed and said she was kidding, but I know she wasn't. She's been pushing me here and there since Benji and I broke up.

Dad changed the subject and talked about all the fun everyone had and how they might make this a monthly thing.

We finished cleaning up and to thank me for my help, they ordered pizza for lunch. We ate around the kitchen island, wrapped up and parted ways.

Hunter texted me back, he hoped the party wasn't too boring.

Yikes.

I replied, "Nah it wasn't too bad".

Eventually further into the conversation he asked if I was going to be around this evening since "I missed out last night".

I joked with him a little but told him I would be and to just come on by when he was free. I did need to re up on weed anyway.

Forward on with the day, I smoked and scrubbed the place. Had to get the scent of Austin out.

Not like I had a whole lot to do, but you know a little laundry here and some cleaning there; I take my time especially when I'm high.

I couldn't stop thinking about last night. I used my vibrating bullet while I finished cleaning, though I teased myself for way too long. I leaned over the counter and finished myself off. When I finally came, I was so wet I had surprised myself.

Before I could catch my breath, I heard a knock at the door. I hadn't been looking at my phone to see that Hunter texted me he was on the way with my weed.

I turned the remote off, but I didn't get to turn the actual bullet itself off. I also wasn't paying attention and left the remote on the counter. I answered the door, and he was like, "Damn, what happened to you", I explained I had been cleaning so I didn't catch his text that he was heading this way.

He followed me to the kitchen telling me how clean my place looked and joked that he wishes his was as clean. He almost instantly found the remote. Somehow when he turned it on and heard it, he knew exactly where it was coming from. He flashed me this devilish grin and told me to tell him what I was really doing.

He backed me up against a wall and before his body could touch mine, I told him, I said "I was really cleaning, I just have my way of making it a more enjoyable experience".

He flipped between settings to see which one got to me the most.

I joked and told him if I knew he was coming, I would have waited. He locked eyes with me and told me he was glad I didn't.

He asked me how wet I was, I told him to see for himself. So, he gets on his knees, pulls down my shorts, put his lips right against mine and makes out with my pussy until I came.

He liked how wet I was, it must be his kink or something… I don't know, but he was really into it. Looking down watching this guy on his knees FOR ME, was unreal.

After he stood up, he flashed those emerald green eyes at me as he wiped his mouth clean. I had to remind myself to breathe.

He told me he really wanted to "finish me off" but he was just here to drop the weed because he had to get to work. He told me he was going to have blue balls his entire shift, so I better be ready for when he gets back here tonight.

I nodded. He left and I took a shower. Now you find me here.

I mean really, what the hell is happening here?!

This stuff happens to everyone else, not me. I am literally juggling two guys right now! Well, I mean Austin and I are just friends, but we have a sexual tension going on between us that's hard to ignore.

Yes, we did just clear that up, I think, but then again Hunter and I are also friends who have a sexual tension going on between us that we agreed to explore… Fuck, I'm juggling between two guys right now.

Talk about a coincidence… I checked my phone and Austin had texted me asking if I wanted to check out a race with him tomorrow. Wasn't one of his but thought I might enjoy it. I told him I would tag along.

About two hours after dinner, Hunter came by, and I had a joint ready for us with some weed cooking show playing in the background. He came straight from work and was covered in food, smelled exactly like a kitchen, burnt grease and all.

Of course, I gave him hell for that. I was wearing a tank top, no bra, a cardigan, and my silky sweatpants, look-in all cozy cute.

After a few hits in, I was sure he was feeling as good as I was. We finally started making out and exploring each other's bodies.

I gave him head while he was sitting on the couch, and he pounded me as I was bent over the kitchen table.

Talk about a tippy toe dance, he's so much fucking taller than I am.

We finished with my legs over his shoulders and his hands tightly gripped around my waist. It was fantastic. We cleaned ourselves up and hung out in the kitchen sipping on some water for a minute.

We got to talking about the 4th of July, the plans are to float down a river during the day and watch the fireworks on a boat at night.

I confessed my fear of water, he laughed, but told me it was fine because it's totally safe and the water is manageable. He promised he wouldn't let anything bad happen to me.

When talking about who would be there, he said it's a small crowd and there's going to be some other girl's there that he will introduce me to.

He asked me if I had ever been on a boat… which was also a hard no. He then told me that I've been sheltered all my life, and to say yes because I'll have a good time.

He left about twenty minutes later.

I have some outfits I need to plan and maybe some shopping to do...

Either way I need to prepare.

I know nothing about any of the people I'll be meeting, and girls can be cruel.

Obviously, I had to call Scarlett, but I was not going to tell her about Austin.

We talked for two hours, and she gave me all the details. I'll be ready and hopefully I can make some friends, maybe some girlfriends this time.

Entry #23

SUNDAY JUNE 30TH 2013

I WOKE UP AND DID MY MORNING ROUTINE. MET AUSTIN AROUND NOON AT THE racetrack. Two of his friends were racing and he was sitting in the stands with their wives cheering them on. I was a little curious why he wasn't racing but I didn't want to pry in case something had happened.

Also, the races were such an adrenaline rush, and it was a serious turn on; I definitely want to go back. And if I get to watch Austin race… holy shit that would be amazing.

The wives seemed pretty cool; we talked a bit throughout the day. We exchanged numbers and started a group chat.

Curious to see how this will go; I'm staying positive.

After the race was over, we decided to head to the bar nearby for some celebratory drinks.

Austin and I were teased for being the only "non couple, couple"; his friends thought we were together, but Austin shut them down. I backed him up like the good friend I am.

We got to know one another over the course of a few hours. We suddenly needed food to soak up the alcohol, so we were there for quite a bit.

It was honestly a fun time, and they're cool people. It's nice to be around positive healthy people for a change.

We called it quits a little after eight and went our separate ways; Austin walked me to my car, and we talked for a minute.

We hugged and went our separate ways. He didn't try to kiss me or anything; I mean, why would he?

I went home and drew myself a bath.

Threw in some pink Himalayan Sea salt, dried rose petals, and a blue sparkly CBD bath bomb for some added flair.

Closing out a long week; my body needed nourishment.

Entry #24

MONDAY JULY 1ˢᵀ 2013

I WOKE UP TO A "GOOD MORNING" TEXT FROM AUSTIN. HE TOLD ME HIS FRIENDS really enjoyed getting to know me and hopes we can all hang out again sometime soon. I responded and told him how sweet that was and that I would be down to hangout again. He didn't text me back, but I saw that he read the message. Probably got busy at work.

I went on with my day and decided to drive out to this lake I had discovered scrolling through social media; it was only a thirty-minute drive, so not too bad. The humidity unfortunately sucked, but there was a decent breeze blowing to make up for it.

I walked alongside the lake for about an hour before I found a tree to rest underneath. I munched on some snacks and played a little music, it was peaceful… Until I got scared by a bee, so I got the fuck away and continued walking.

A few people were out and about so I put my headphones in and did my thing. I even found some honeysuckle! It made me miss home for a bit… we had honeysuckle growing in our neighbors' yard and she would always let me pick at some so I could get a little taste.

Her name was Ginny, and she was the sweetest old lady… it was really hard on the parents when she passed away.

Gosh, so much has changed.

▪▪▪

Hunter texted me, he was bored at work wondering what I was up to, so I sent him a picture of the lake. Turns out he used to go fishing here with some friends during his high school summer days. We texted a little back and forth, but I was really captivated by what was in front of me so I may have taken a little longer in between responding.

I also found these pretty pink flowers, no idea what the hell they're called, but they smelled almost like roses but a little sweeter if that makes sense, so I broke one off and took it back home with me. Kind of makes me want to start growing some plants of my own, but maybe I'll save that for later when I'm ready to take on that commitment… I don't exactly have a strong knack for keeping plants alive.

Oh! Hear me out… I'm thinking of getting a tattoo! I don't know what I want yet, but I know I want something. Going to explore it a little more, but hoping Austin may be able to point me in the right direction given he's the only person I know here with tattoos. We shall see!

Entry #25

WEDNESDAY JULY 3RD 2013

OKAY, TECHNICALLY IT'S AFTER MIDNIGHT SO IT'S THURSDAY, BUT I'LL LET IT slide. It's not the new day until I go to sleep and wake up to it, anyway.

Hunter and I just went for a late-night walk.

He texted me around eleven or so asking what I was up to, turns out he couldn't sleep either, so we decided to go for a walk.

We made our way to the treehouse, and I immediately headed towards the swings.

I fucking love swing sets.

We passed a joint back and forth until it started to rain!

We took cover in the treehouse (there's a small section with a roof).

Getting caught in the rain created some kind of vibe. It was a little cramped and I was on top the whole time, but we made it work and christened the treehouse.

Crossing treehouse sex off my nonexistent bucket list.

There was finally a break in the rain, so we figured that was the best time to leave. He insisted on walking me home, I told him not to, so he didn't get rained on again, but he followed me anyway. It started to down pour, so I drove him home.

He looks cute when he's wet. Kept his hat on the whole time, too.

I parked and we sat in the car for a minute. He thanked me for the ride even though he wouldn't have minded the walk. I told him if he wasn't letting me walk alone in the rain then I wouldn't let him do it either.

He leaned in and kissed me goodnight. I suddenly found myself wishing I was going inside with him so we could get undressed and go to bed together.

I think I might be into him for real… I hope he doesn't find out. While it wouldn't be the worst thing in the world, having to reject him would be…

Remember, you packed your life up and moved across the country for a fresh start. You didn't move down here just to end up in a relationship.

Entry # 26

YESTERDAY WAS… A LOT OF FUN!

Floating down a river is actually not half bad and way more enjoyable than the beach. The water wasn't too horrible; nobody died and nothing gross or scary disturbed me.

I was lucky and didn't get too drunk… floating on the water really makes time slow down enough to not realize how many drinks you've had, until you're puking over the edge of your float.

Thankfully I wasn't the one who did that, I played it safe and hydrated constantly. I was serious about wanting to make a good first impression if you couldn't already tell.

His friends were cool, and their girlfriends were cool too. I seemed to have a lot in common with them; we exchanged numbers and started a group chat.

About three quarters of the way through the float, we stopped at this island so we could eat, smoke, and chill for a sec.

I was dead ass high in the middle of a large body of water held up by only a small floatie, paranoid as fuck, because I can't swim the greatest.

Hunter and I floated next to each other for the rest of the way. We had an honest conversation, got to know one another better.

I still haven't told him about my health and the car accident settlement.

By the time the float was over, I could not have been more excited to get the fuck home so I could shower.

Everyone went their separate ways, though a little birdie followed me home, and we showered together.

After we finished, he went in the kitchen and made us some coffee while I dried my hair and did my makeup, still wrapped in a towel, as was he.

We chatted and sipped our coffees as we both got ready for the evening.

I caught him watching me get ready and I tried so hard not to look back at him myself, mostly because I was blushing like crazy knowing he was watching me. I shut the bathroom door so I could put my dress on, though.

It was perfect for the evening. I put on an A-line, V-neck, mint blue floral boho summer dress; It had a little ruffle to it and came with pockets and a light brown belt. I paired it with some wedges.

That was the first time Hunter had really seen me "dressed up". Usually we're dressed down or naked, so it was nice to clean up this time.

He looked me up and down and told me I looked pretty. He looked pretty good himself, despite wearing the usual jeans and T-shirt look.

He looks <u>incredible</u> in jeans.

We drove together since it "made more sense" and were the last to show up. Everyone looked amazing, but I'm obsessing over myself right now because I've never worn a dress like this before… usually I'd cover up or whatever.

Dude, the boat was huge… more like a mini yacht. It had two levels and could sleep eight people.

Everyone got super drunk, and we scattered when it was time to watch the fireworks. Hunter and I weren't the only single people there, so not having that pressure was nice.

While I talked with some of the girlfriends a lot, we did stay pretty close to each other for the most part of the night.

I love fireworks. Watching them can be so romantic, especially when you're sitting on the edge of a boat, next to a cute guy, watching them glimmer over the ocean. It was something I had never seen before; I've only seen fireworks shot over a field.

Since we agreed to no sleepovers, we had no choice but to get ourselves home. He had a little too much to drink, so I drove his jeep to get us some food and took him home.

I learned a little more about him. He owns the house he lives in; his grandparents had paid it off and left it to him when they passed away. He has a roommate for the extra cash; since he works a lot and goes to school full time, he's not really there much anyway.

I helped him inside and got him to his room; he wasn't plastered but he definitely needed some guidance. I got him settled and walked home.

I didn't mind the walk, he's barely five minutes from me.

By the time I got home, settled in bed myself, it was almost three in the morning, I was exhausted.

I slept in until noon. I woke up and had a text from Hunter thanking me for getting us home safely last night. He felt horrible I had to walk home alone in the middle of the night, but I really didn't mind. He told me he owed me one and he really appreciated it.

It rained all day, and I did actually have sunburn, so I had a lazy day on the couch. Smoked, read, ate, watched tv, and that was about it.

Texted with Scarlett a bit to keep her updated on Hunter and me… I wonder if he's going to tell her brother about last night.

Austin texted me for the 4th and I wished him a happy one back. He asked me what I was up to, and he left me on read after I told him I was hanging out with some new friends I made. I did ask what he was up to, so maybe he got distracted. Not going to look into it too much.

Entry # 27

I DON'T KNOW WHAT THE FUCK HAPPENED, BUT I FELT LIKE TOTAL DOG SHIT yesterday and it kind of makes me feel sad because I haven't felt sick like that in a long time.

I wonder if maybe it was too much sun from the river or maybe I was dehydrated? I don't know, but I am making it a priority to drink more water each day so that should help…. I'm just glad to be feeling better today, I was a little worried.

Any who.

I was craving sweets, so I ran to the grocery store for supplies and spent my afternoon baking cupcakes and chocolate chip cookies. The cookies were my favorite to make… my entire apartment smelled of sugar and vanilla so now I need to find some scented candles that smell like cookies.

The cupcakes on the other hand… I accidentally burned them, and the smoke detector went off… I smoked a little too much weed and forgot to set a timer, so by the time I remembered I was making cupcakes, it was a little too late… let's just say it's been about two hours and my place still smells like smoke and burnt chocolate… so gross and such a waste, but at least I got some cookies out of it.

Hunter texted me wanting to swing by after work, I wasn't really feeling up for company, but I let him come over anyway.

He teased me about the burnt cupcakes, but he made up for it when he ate me out on the couch, so.

We did end up having sex after that, but that's not the part I want to write about.

When we were done fooling around, we were standing in the kitchen passing a bowl back and forth munching on some cookies when he suddenly stops, looks me straight in the face and wipes chocolate off the corner of my mouth.

I froze. I was so embarrassed.

I couldn't believe he did that; just seemed so… intimate? I don't know. I just had all these feelings rush through me after he did that and I tried really hard not to blush, but I did, and of course he noticed.

He asked me why I was blushing so hard; I didn't know what to say so I just told him he caught me off guard and changed the subject.

It was ten something at night, so I blamed it on the fact that I skipped dinner. He offered to order us a pizza, but I declined and found a way to part ways for the night.

...

I need to be careful before I fall too hard for this guy. Boundaries can be healthy if handled correctly, so I need to shift my focus in that direction.

Why does he have to be so fucking attractive?

Entry #28

WEDNESDAY JULY 10TH 2013

BEING IN A GROUP CHAT WITH WIVES AND ANOTHER WITH GIRLFRIENDS IS totally and completely different, yo. Like I've got the best of both worlds.

I've been out shopping with the wives, at the beach with the girlfriends. A little bar hopping here and there.

Though I guess it really doesn't matter anymore because it's in the past, I do need to acknowledge that I was not having this much fun back home.

I had all these friends, yet I still felt lonely. I barely know anyone here and I'm happier than I've been in a long time.

Makes me wonder if things took a turn when Benji and I broke up… after all our history involved mutual friends… maybe after the breakup they chose sides, I don't know. I do know I'm not going to stress myself over the past anymore if I can help it.

I have to say, I'm enjoying this new version of myself and it's nice being able to share my story the way I want, instead of someone else telling it for me. I've come a long way; I deserve to be proud of my success.

I've been hanging by the pool and riding my bike a lot lately, it's nice having my own routine and to be truthful I'll miss it when I start working again, but nothing beats making money, so I'll live. I bet I'll use the elliptical a lot more then too… right now it's just good for rainy days or when it's too hot out, I love my bike.

Austin told me a little bit about what he does at work, and it sounds as stressful as Mom had mentioned. Apparently, the pay has the potential to be great, but I didn't need him to tell me that… I mean look at the house Mom bought all on her own.

While I look forward to what's ahead, I'm going to make sure I enjoy the time I have now. I need to remind myself that it's okay to live in the present. My past is what got me here and my future doesn't exist yet. If I'm constantly thinking about one over the other, I'm going to miss out on what's happening now, right in front of me.

It may look a little different than I had imagined, but it's opening life up to possibilities I never saw coming. I think that's the greatest gift I could have ever been given… a second chance.

Hunter came over after work and we had sex within minutes of him walking in the door; he had a rough shift at work and needed to relieve some stress.

We smoked and got stupid high together on the couch. He thanked me again for getting us home on the 4th and apologized for getting too drunk and not being able to drive us home. I was surprised he was still hung up on that, but I assured him it was fine. We relaxed on the couch until he started falling asleep, we parted ways, and now here I am.

Anxiety struck me and I wondered if I satisfied him the way he did me.

I mean he wouldn't have sex with me if he didn't want to so what the fuck am I so paranoid about. I wish I could blame it on the weed but this time it's that good ole anxiety.

That is exactly why I don't want to be in a relationship right now. I don't want to feel anxious for no reason and worry about someone's opinion of me more than how I feel myself; I mean it's pathetic.

I know I need to be easy on myself, but I also need to make sure I don't put myself in the same position I was in before. I am a person just as much as the guy I'm dating, and I deserve to take care of myself too.

Now, Benji wasn't all bad, I loved him and a part of me probably always will, I just couldn't be the person he wanted me to be. I've spent so much of my life prioritizing everything around me; I lost sight of what I want.

But I can protect myself now. I've started punching back, and for real this time.

$\mathcal{E}$ntry # 29

TODAY WAS COOL, WENT FOR A NICE BIKE RIDE AND USED EVERY SINGLE HAIR and skin care product I own when I showered. Even moisturized when I got out. I guess you can say I was definitely feeling myself.

Hunter unexpectedly got the night off (there was a small grease fire, and they had to shut down the place for the night), so he invited me to a bonfire on the beach the boat friend was hosting. (His friends' parents are loaded, they've got a beach house they let him use).

He picked me up and we rode together… it's only a matter of time before someone questions it. I mean we are technically neighbors, so, that's a good cover, I guess.

Anyway, I wore shorts, a green bralette, and a gray zippered hoodie. He wore shorts and a red T-shirt. Had his hat on again, front facing, and like usual, he looked really good.

He's so sexy when he drives.

He had one hand on the steering wheel and the other on the gear shift. I fantasized about placing my hand over his, before reality hit me and I remembered friends didn't do that.

The crowd was small, only about a dozen people or so, which was great. Got to chill with the girlfriends for a bit and gossiped. They finally asked me if I was dating Hunter, I told them we were just hanging out and brought up how we connected. Thankfully that was enough to satisfy their curiosity.

Hunter and I drank a little, but mostly smoked so we could drive home.

At one point we took a walk along the shoreline and for maybe five seconds, our pinkies intertwined before we caught ourselves and let go.

We left around ten and he took me home. The lights were off when we pulled up, so the parents must have called an early night.

I was feeling brave, so I told him to turn off the jeep and the lights.

I took full control; leaned over, grabbed him by his shirt and pulled him in close to kiss him. It was hard to make out like that, so he moved his seat back and I climbed on top of him. I unzipped my hoodie so he could catch the full view.

We totally had sex. In his jeep, right in front of the house… parents could have opened a window or something literally at any given moment.

Their bedroom window faces the front of the house for fucks sake.

But none of that mattered; I was living in the moment enjoying every second of it.

Thankfully we had a condom nearby, cause pulling out wasn't going to happen in the cramped position we were in. He drives a jeep, but still.

We talked for a minute before calling it a night. I washed up and immediately put pen to paper.

This doesn't really surprise me to say, but I'm totally and completely into him... I have feelings for my weed dealer.

Good thing we agreed on boundaries so early in the beginning… Who knew I would need them most.

I need to check myself and re-focus my priorities.

Entry # 30

I TEXTED AUSTIN DURING BOOTY CALL HOURS LAST NIGHT, ASKING IF HE wanted to meet up for lunch to tell me more about work, so I could prepare myself.

Refocusing my priorities back over to myself.

He too was up late and responded fairly quickly. Surprised he was free on such short notice, but we decided on noon and said goodnight.

When I met up with him, I was armed with a notebook and pen, I told him to tell me everything.

He teased me about my enthusiasm and told me to relax.

He was sweet; he gave me exactly what I asked for. My hand hurt from writing so much, apparently that was the point and that's why he told me to relax… While it's nice to get a head start on the basics and terminology, the rest is better learned in person.

Which explained the specific two-week extensive shadowing Mom was putting me through before she'd teach me anything.

Holy fuck. It just occurred to me that I don't know who I'll be shadowing for those two weeks. Fucking better be Mom.

We stayed until we realized it was nearly dinner time. We talked for five hours.

I felt bad for keeping him so long on his day off talking about work. He said he didn't mind because he likes what he does, but, if I wanted to make it up to him, I could have dinner with him.

He's such a charmer. Southern boys are dangerous.

When suggesting dinner places, he mentioned Japanese; it's his absolute favorite so he took me to this hole in the wall place that was fairly empty when we got there. He assured me it was the best… and it was.

Talking over dinner was different than lunch because we weren't talking about work, he asked me how my summer was going and if I was having any fun.

I mean I am having fun, so I wasn't lying, I just didn't include in my recap of festivities that I was sleeping with my weed dealer.

I did thank him again for introducing me to the wives, I told him we've gone out a couple of times and he was happy I made friends.

I then awkwardly pointed out how much he's done for me… I mean he introduced me to some of his friends and spent an entire Saturday explaining to me what he does for work. I told him I felt like I owed him big time, so he told me I could make it up to him when I come to work for Mom. He's so sure I'm going to fall in love with the job and want to stay on for a permanent position. I'm open to any and all possibilities, so we'll see.

Turns out some of the positions open involve working underneath his super vision. Meaning he would be my boss…

I asked him to elaborate on how exactly I would make it up to him at work, and he told me to get my mind out of the gutter because he's talking about having me do the work he doesn't like to do.

Whoops.

I changed the subject and asked him how his summer was going and if he was having fun; considering we're supposed to be on similar journeys.

He told me he's exploring yoga and meditation right now, which I thought was pretty cool. He showed me this app he uses, and it made me realize I rarely use mine.

He told me about a class he takes every week and offered the information if I ever wanted to go sometime. Not with him, but in general. I caught that.

We eventually finished our food and decided there was nowhere else to go but home.

He walked me to my car, gave me a nice big hug, and we parted ways.

I learned a lot of information and I have more work to do than I expected before I step my foot in the door. I spent the rest of my evening turning my notes into flash cards and composing study guides.

Entry # 31

SUNDAY MORNING BREAKFAST WITH THE PARENTS. THIS TIME MOM MADE A quiche; eggs for the base, some cheese, bacon, and ham… it was so good.

We talked about current events, I left out a few key parts to my summer fun, but all in all it sounds like we're all having a great time here.

Mom mentioned some family would be visiting, but not until Thanksgiving… of course everyone is coming here, so that should be interesting. Though that's four months away, so I'm not going to bother with it right now.

After breakfast I felt energized, decided to go on a bike trail. Despite the incredible weather we were having, there was nobody around; I had free range. I cruised through the late morning summer breeze and listened to every random song that played on my playlist, didn't skip once.

I had no idea where the trail was taking me, but I felt amazing and that's all I cared about.

About two miles in I got a phone call, it was Hunter. He had the day off and was wondering if we could finish the conversation we started Friday.

I was too busy with Austin yesterday; I didn't text Hunter back…

I almost forgot that it was me who made the first move… so I told him where I was, and he came and met me. We met up at a bench in front of a lake and passed a joint back and forth.

Love how he's always prepared.

About four puffs in, he broke the ice about Friday night and told me that I could take over the driver's seat whenever I wanted. I laughed and told him I didn't know what was in me to do what I did; he responded by telling me he likes knowing I do crazy things around him.

I changed the subject and brought the focus back to the bike ride we were supposed to be on. We did about twelve miles in total.

I still can't believe he tagged along with me.

We went back to my place, and we showered together.

He stunk of sweat. Couldn't tell ya why but it was workin for me.

The parents were out for a bit, so I wasn't worried about them seeing his jeep.

Both starving after biking for so many miles, we had sandwiches delivered and relaxed on the couch.

Smoked of course, just got lost relaxing and following along with whatever was on tv. We fell asleep together. Must have smoked an indica.

I woke up and it was a little after seven; he was spooning me. I carefully got up so I could pee, and I think it woke him up because I found him up and stretching when I returned.

He reached so tall, his shirt lifted up, and I saw his happy trail.

He caught me looking at him and asked me what I was looking at.

I said, "Obviously you."

He looks so sexy when he first wakes up…

I walked up to him, and I traced my finger up and down the center of his chest.

I slid his pants down, took him by his arms, and pushed him down onto the couch.

I took everything but my bra off, and I climbed on top of him.

I kissed his neck; He took his shirt off.

He balled my hair up in a fist while I fucked him on the couch. He grabbed my ass so hard he probably left a mark.

He was giggly after, he was like, "So, where'd that come from? I'm digging this spark of yours right now."

I said, "I don't know, just something about the way you looked when you were stretching made me want you right then and there."

Literally his response was a smile followed by, "Do you want to go get something to eat?"

Weird, but sure.

He took me to this place a few blocks away. It was difficult holding back how much fun I was having with him… I mean we basically spent an entire day together.

I was in my head while we were eating, and he could tell, so he asked me what I was thinking about.

You, duh.

I froze, I didn't know what to say. I had to come up with something quick.

I broke one of our rules, I lied and told him I was feeling a bit homesick lately. He told me sweet things to help me feel better which was nice. Aside from the weed and sex, he really is a sweet guy.

We finished and he drove me home. I thought about him the entire way back.

When he dropped me off, we didn't kiss goodbye or anything. I think that was the slap from reality I needed to remember that we're just friends casually hooking up with each other; nothing more, nothing less… besides him also being my weed dealer.

Today was fun; No pressure, no expectations, and that's the way it needs to stay.

Entry # 32

HUNTER TEXTED ME THIS MORNING THAT HE WAS SORE, 'IN MORE WAYS THAN he liked' and asked why I biked so much. I told him I did it because it makes me feel good.

We ended up sexting

All.

Day.

Long.

He had to work a double, so the tension was pretty painful until he was finally able to swing by after work.

He stunk of burnt kitchen grease and sweat.

He walked in the door and told me to take my clothes off. I didn't react.

He called me by my name!

He goes, "Lucy, I told you to take your clothes off".

I responded by rolling my eyes and saying, "Okay. But only if you take off yours".

Fuck, I love his hair, but I wish he had his hat on.

He nodded in agreement, and we slowly undressed right there in the living room.

He took me by my wrists and slowly backed me up against my front door.

He raised my arms above my head and held them there while he looked me up and down. It made me so nervous I could feel his eyes studying every inch of me. I don't know how tall he is, but he's tall enough to tower over me.

I felt insecure in my own body. As I reflect back, I don't know why I was feeling that way… especially in that moment. Not like Hunter makes me feel bad about myself or anything, I guess I just haven't been looked at in that way by anyone other than Benji… and he and I were in love.

Hunter caught on that I was feeling some type of way, so he checked in to make sure I was cool.

He has this way of knowing when I'm in my head… why would he pay attention to something like that?

I told him we were good, so we returned to the heat of the moment like nothing had happened.

He told me how amazing my body looks.

I then became even more awkward and nervous, so I giggled, and he giggled, all while I was freaking out on the inside.

He drops my arms and traces his hand down the center of my chest. Cups the boobs on his way down, of course.

He totally went to town on my pussy; I'm talking lips, tongue, fingers… over and over until I finally came. He recently cut his hair, it wasn't as long as it normally is, so I wasn't sure what to do with my hands. I just held his head, I guess.

I took his hand and walked him to my bedroom. He just wanted to be inside me, so I got on top for a minute or two before he took over and had me on all fours.

Not to compare, but to compare. I never did anything like this with Benji, we just fooled around a little and had sex. I'm kind of digging the idea that I can finally express myself sexually and feel comfortable about it after.

We finished and he soon after went on his way home. I took a shower and well, here I am. It's confusing to think that he may actually be helping me grow as a person. Is that even a thing?

Where are you going with this, Lucy?

$\mathcal{E}$ntry # 33

MONDAY JULY 22ND 2013

OKAY, SO I KNOW I AM A LITTLE BEHIND, WHILE I DON'T LOVE MISSING DETAILS, I've been busy and haven't been able to write. Busy doing fun things.

I did also finally find a good waxing spa! Still hurts like a bitch but the lady who owns the place is cool.

On a not so fun note, I don't hear from anyone back home anymore, I stopped reaching out first- I was tired of the one-sided friendships, and it's never been clearer now that I've moved away that things were never as great as they seemed.

Scarlett and I still talk, but not as much as we used to and it kind of sucks, I miss my best friend, but I guess that's what happens when one of you moves away. Out of sight, out of mind.

Now that we got the lame sad stuff out of the way, let's talk about the fun stuff. THE HIGHLIGHTS if you will.

Hunter invited me to a cooking class, he said he won it in a raffle at work and had a feeling I might be into it. It was totally random and out of the blue, but I secretly loved every minute of it. We made homemade pasta, sauce, and tiramisu for dessert.

The class ended when the food came out of the oven, so everyone stood around and ate at their counters.

We make a good team.

We packed up our leftovers and he walked me over to my car.

We drove here separately, by the way. Not that either of us asked to ride together, I just told him I would meet him there.

Keeping it casual.

He asked me if I wanted to smoke. I really wanted to, but not when I had to immediately drive after. He countered my no and asked if I wanted to go back to his place instead… he added that his roommate was out of town.

Of course, I wanted to go, considering he knows my place like the back of his hand, I was curious to know more about him.

We hung out in the living room smoking and watching tv. He was on one end of the couch, and I was on the other.

Couldn't tell ya how it started, but we had sex and 69'd on the couch.

Stoned sex is the best sex.

I got dressed and freshened up in the bathroom. I figured I should maybe go.

I didn't want to, I just thought we reached that point in the night. I mean he hangs around after sometimes but then sometimes he doesn't.

Thankfully he probably saw me in my head, so he took control and asked me if I wanted my leftovers heated up.

Back to the living room we went, eating pasta close to midnight.

We noticed the time when it popped on the tv, and I mentioned I should probably head out.

He said, "Sure, or you could stay the night".

Was he really implying we should break one of our rules? Should I have called him out on it? Probably. Was I going to? Absolutely not.

I fought with myself in my head because I literally just recently, reminded myself that I needed to pull myself together. But I wanted this, and I told myself I'd live in the moment.

Before I could have the chance to respond, he offered me a T-shirt and sweatpants so I could be more comfortable. Ha.

We've laid in bed together before, but this was different. This was the first time we'd been in his bed, aside from the time I brought him home on the 4th.

The only guy I've ever spent the night with before was Benji, and he and I were serious. Hunter and me? We're just… really good friends who hook up for fun.

We made it through five minutes of searching for a movie to put on, before we just played something in the background so we could fool around.

I didn't think my sexual energy could be matched, and here he is placing a check mate on my ass.

We took our time exploring each other's body and it's not something we did often. I didn't want to overthink things, but it might be a little too late for that.

Obviously, the sex was fucking incredible, always is.

Our bodies are in sync with one another, that's the best way to describe it. We read each other well.

Neither one of us mentioned the fact that we were intentionally breaking one of our rules. I wonder who's going to mention it first.

The next morning wasn't so bad, I woke up to him showering so I got myself situated when he came out all shower fresh, wrapped in a towel from the waist down asking me if I wanted to get food.

I don't know what soap he uses, but he smelled fantastic.

I always want food, but I also like to be showered and smell good too, especially when I'm around the guy I'm sleeping with.

I improvised. I used his mouth wash, then remembered I had a small deodorant in my bag, so I was safe. I also found some emergency perfume I had hidden with the deodorant; smelled like fruit and flowers.

We smoked before we left, and he drove us to some breakfast café.

I wanted to sarcastically bring up how this was the longest time we had spent together, but I was worried about how that would make me look, so I kept it to myself.

He would randomly look up and make eye contact with me while he was eating, and I wanted to melt every single time.

His eyes are my fucking kryptonite.

The ride back was fairly quiet, so he put on the radio… country music of all things.

I told him he had bad taste in music and put on some other random station.

He glanced at me in silence and said he'd get me for that later. Then put back the station he had on and told me it's not polite in the South to touch a man's radio.

The back-and-forth bickering reminded me of Benji and I. Which then reminded me that Hunter and I weren't dating, so I needed to not take everything that happens between us so seriously.

When we got back to his place, I was ready to bounce, and he had to get to work so we called it.

He high fived me as I left. Men are so fucking weird.

I went home and took a shower, napped for like two or three hours. Woke up, had some lunch, and went on about my day.

I've been casually texting more with Austin, though obviously not when I'm with Hunter.

While I am attracted to him, I do support his journey and I don't want to unintentionally get in the way of that. Plus, he's been a great friend to me, so I want to be a great friend back.

Entry #34

I WOKE UP THIS MORNING WITH A TEXT REMINDER THAT I HAVE A DOCTOR'S appointment this Thursday, I forgot I made an appointment before we moved down.

Of course, I'm nervous, but I've been feeling well these past few months and taking things easy.

I decided not to let that anxiety affect my day, so I made some coffee, grabbed a protein muffin, and sat out on the balcony for a bit.

Decided a bike ride would be nice… just didn't expect it to last for three hours. I was totally caught up in the moment and not paying attention to my phone or really where I was; it was peaceful.

I got home a little after five, took a nice dip in the pool and finished up with a steamy shower.

Made dinner and managed to squeeze in some reading… it felt good to get lost behind the pages of a book again. I've been reading work notes a lot lately, so the change was nice.

It's now a little after midnight and there's a slight breeze blowing my hair in the wind. I'm on the balcony writing and it's seventy-two degrees out.

I'm wearing a tank top and shorts, and I've got a joint burning next to me.

I should snap a picture; I feel so sexy right now. Writing is my superpower.

I haven't really processed the fact that Hunter and I spent the night together. I mean to be truthful I knew it was going to happen at some point, I just figured it would have happened… not so soon?

What changed?

I'm sure we'll talk about it but until then, I'm going to overthink things and run multiple scenarios in my head. He made the move, so I'll sit back and let him take the lead on this one. Makes me nervous to say that, but I'm going to go with the flow.

Entry # 35

THURSDAY JULY 25TH 2013

GOT A MANI-PEDI YESTERDAY! ALMOST FORGOT HOW NICE THOSE CAN BE. Texting Hunter as if we didn't just spend the night together.

The new doctor was alright, she's familiar with my medical history and on board with my progress. She asked to run the usual labs and a few others to be safe and that was pretty much the end of that.

All that stress for nothing.

Went on with the rest of my day hanging by the pool texting Austin about yoga and sending nudes to Hunter.

Boundaries are wonderful.

I'm struggling to accept where my life is right now. It's just so different from what I imagined, and to think I hated the thought of moving down here…

If I was home right now, I don't know where I'd be living exactly; maybe in a hotel until I found a stable place? Maybe on a friend's couch or in a spare room? And what about an income? Sure, I have some money right now, but that only lasts for so long.

I almost feel like I'm not being completely honest with the new people in my life.

I'm in new territory and trying to adjust as best I can… I guess you could say I'm not used to this side of the fence. Maybe I've spent so much time watering myself, that I've finally grown into the person I've always wanted to become. Maybe I have a little imposter syndrome happening here too.

I won't know what I don't know until I find out.

Around eleven or so Hunter came by after work, and we smoked on the deck out back (parents are out of town on a business trip until Monday).

We talked for a bit, just checking in kind of conversation to see how the other is doing. I was surprised we didn't talk about our sleepover, but I did well and didn't bring it up.

He's doing well all around, jealous of my free time… I reminded him it's only for the summer and then it's right to work in the Fall. We talked a bit about the job shadowing gig and just whatever else came up from there.

His weed is always strong, but there was something different about it tonight.

Maybe I got too much sun earlier… I don't know, but I was in desperate need to get in the pool.

I just wanted to be in the water, but he took it as an invitation and scooped my ass up. We splashed each other around for a bit and got a little fussy before I got on top and rode him on one of the lawn chairs.

I don't know how he gets me in the positions he does, but he makes it worth it every time.

Totts a new fan favorite sex location, by the way. Who knew. Thank God we don't have security cameras.

We eventually wrapped up our evening and parted ways; I wanted to shower and go to bed, I was shot.

Entry # 36

DUDE.

Hunter has been over after work every night since Thursday.

He spent the night last night, I'm out on the balcony with some coffee right now, he's still in bed. We got super drunk last night, no way he could drive, let alone walk, even if it was just a few houses down.

We played video games, went swimming, had sex in the shower, on the bed, on the couch and the kitchen table at some point.

We've been all over the place.

...

He woke up and found me writing so I had to take a break and come back to this.

He didn't have to work today, so we spent the morning together.

We had some burgers and fries delivered to help with the hangover. Mine wasn't too bad, but enough to notice. I'm sure he felt like hell too, he drank more than I did.

We spent the day on the couch, watched a few episodes until dinner time. He had a craving for steak, so he had some groceries delivered and whipped us up a meal.

Remember, he's the chef so he handles the cooking, I get to sip wine on the counter and slip him sips every time he walks by me. Watching him do something he loves is the kind of foreplay I never knew existed until now.

We ate dinner in the living room with a movie on and called it a night soon after the movie ended.

I didn't want it to end if I'm being honest, but I know it was what needed to happen… we've been spending a lot of time together lately, it was bound to end at some point.

While I've enjoyed the past few days with him, I've been having some fun on my own. Random drives here and there, ten-mile bike rides, getting lost in the pages of good books, pool days and sun tans… Loving life right now.

Entry #37

BESIDES A LITTLE MAINTENANCE TWEAK, MY BLOOD WORK CAME BACK WITHIN ranges they're supposed to be in. I'm relieved that my path of better health is continuing in the right direction. I feel pretty good about myself and while I hope I don't jinx it, I'm enjoying the peace I feel right now.

I had to run by Mom's job to bring her something, of course she asked Austin to give me a tour of the office while I was there. I don't know what was different this time, but as soon as we were behind closed doors, he couldn't kiss me fast enough.

Talk about the timing and location…

It twisted my guts to do it, but I pulled away from him and reminded him where we were and asked what was up… was just a little blindsided is all.

The attitude in the air changed and I somewhat wished I could take back what I said, but it needed to be done.

He apologized and said he didn't know what he was thinking, and he didn't mean to make things weird.

I told him it was fine, and I asked if he wanted to talk about it, but he assured me he was cool. We pretty much finished up the tour and went our separate ways from there.

It's been roughly two weeks since we've last seen each other and while we have been texting, it's been mostly about work stuff and random chatting here and there. Was I giving off a vibe or something?

I've been talking about myself and the men too much, it's time to chime in on a new friend I've made. Well, it's one of the girlfriends from the group, her name's Hazel.

Turns out she's a stoner too, so I went by her place after the office, and we smoked so much weed. She and I are the only two in the group that smoke, so it's nice to have another stoner chick to chill with. I'm not exactly sure, but I believe we're about the same age. She does some type of work with health insurance claims.

We were too high to drive so we had some pizza delivered.

OMG it smelled so good. They cooked it to perfection! The crust was crispy when I folded it and the pepperoni masked the entire smell of the pizza.

She gave me the inside scoop on some of the other girls in the group and I learned all the drama. She asked me how I knew Hunter, so I told her the story. She asked me what I thought of him, and I told her he was cool and all, but we were just friends. She pushed a little, but I didn't budge. I'm still getting to know her so I need to know I can trust her before I spill my secrets. She did give me the inside scoop on him though; she said he's a really solid guy and absolutely the kind of person you want in your corner, dating or not. That was nice to hear.

After like eleven or so, I headed home and took a shower. Got caught up in here and now I'm pretty much chillin in bed with some random tv show playing in the background.

Today was a day. But it was a day I put my needs first. Austin threw me a curve ball I did not see coming and while he said he's cool, I should still probably check in with him. I do care for him as a friend.

Entry #38

IT RAINED ALLLLLLL DAY YESTERDAY. I WAS RELIEVED I DIDN'T HAVE TO GO anywhere; it was so nasty out. I was snuggled up with a blanket and watched cheesy rom coms all day.

It was fairly crappy out today, so I decided to treat myself and made chicken parmesan for dinner, with a side of wine. By the time dinner was ready I was about a bottle in and feeling free. I sat at the table, lit a candle, and played a movie in the background while I ate.

About three or so hours later I laid in bed just chillin with a movie on texting Hunter, sobering up. He asked if I was up for some company, and I told him I could be if he convinced me I needed any.

This mother fucker called me up on the phone and I had no idea what to expect, we usually only text when we're not together. His accent is one thing, but how he sounds on the phone is an entirely different story.

Brought me back to the first time I talked to him on Xbox.

He doesn't even need to say anything sexual to turn me on. I love his voice and the flow of his words.

He eased his way into asking me all these intrusive questions - about what I was wearing, how I was feeling… He lowered his voice and spoke more softly. He talked about what he was up to in <u>very</u> specific detail.

I was wrapped around his finger, and he'd barely said anything to me yet.

He pushed things a little further, stayed there for a minute then continued down this rabbit hole of unexpected, but welcomed, nasty sex talk.

He asked if the front door was unlocked, usually it's not unless I know someone is coming over.

This mother fucker knocked on the door and told me over the phone to let him inside. He drove over here knowing he was going to get some; I mean he was right, so I wasn't mad; the confidence and foreplay was hot.

Though, I decided to play him at his own game, so I answered the door completely naked.

He responded by grabbing me by my throat and slowly backing me up onto the kitchen table where he ate me out before he even took his shoes off.

We eventually made our way to bed, and I think I twisted myself in three or so different positions before we finished.

I don't know what was with him, but he had a thirst he was trying to quench, and I was happy to be on the receiving end of that.

We puffed on the joint I rolled earlier and chilled in bed for a few minutes. It was quiet until he teased me about the way I sound on the phone, he said my accent is so thick he can't get enough of it. I laughed and told him his did the trick for me too.

We laid on our sides facing each other with one arm rested under our head, and the other passing the joint back and forth. It was so chill I hadn't acknowledged the fact that we were both still naked until now.

I was fucking blitzed, and I know he was too, he played some music on his phone, and we talked about whatever random thought came to mind. The no pressure vibe was nice.

We cozied up and I rested my head on his chest; he laid there with his hands folded up behind his head, flexing those juicy arms of his.

He smelled good. Like, he has a sweet scent, a manly sweet scent. I wonder if it's his deodorant or something.

We laid there in silence listening to music. A little intimate if you look back on it, but I'm glad I lived in the moment and enjoyed it instead of trying to process or define it.

It was about four in the morning when I woke up and caught the time; we totally fell asleep. I bounced back and forth about the idea of the parents seeing his jeep here in the morning.

I couldn't sleep, I was so nervous; I woke up at like seven something and snuck into the bathroom to take a shower.

Hunter woke up and joined me…

I was wrapped up in a towel brushing my teeth and putting makeup on when I caught him watching me as he was getting dressed. I felt a little shy but asked him what he was looking at and he said, "Obviously you".

He had to head out to get to work. Both Mom and Dad were home, so I'm sure I'll probably hear about this later.

When we said goodbye, I was still in a towel as I led him out the door. While I understood why there was no huge or glamorous goodbye, a part of me was still hoping for one. I wonder if he could tell.

He left and I went on with my day, made some bacon and waffles for breakfast. Mom texted me around lunch asking if I had dinner plans and I thought well fuck, here we go.

Dad was hosting a poker night at the house, so she wanted to get out and give him space.

We met up at seven and drove together, ended up at a pizzeria that smelled like WAY too much garlic.

After about an hour and two drinks in, she finally asks me who spent the night. I told her it was an accident; she didn't care one bit; she was just curious to see who I've met here. So, I told her about Hunter, not about the sex obviously, I told her he sells me weed and we've become friends and that he's introduced me to some friends I've made.

She then immediately asked me about Austin (which is becoming a pattern) … I told her we were just friends and that he also introduced me to some people.

I flat out asked her why she was so obsessed with me dating him; she said she didn't mean to put that on me, she just thinks he's a great guy and would treat me well. Despite the fact that he could be my boss, she assured me she wouldn't put me on his team. But she isn't opposed to healthy office romance.

Uh.

I told her how much I appreciated her looking out for me but that I'm focusing on myself for the time being and a relationship wasn't high on the list of things I wanted. She understood, but also reminded me that it's okay to have a little fun. She gave me the sex wink and we busted out laughing.

It was nice to have dinner together and I hope we do it more often. We got home around ten and that was about it.

Entry #39

MONDAY AUGUST 5TH 2013

WASN'T A TERRIBLE WEEKEND; HUNG OUT AND WENT TO A BAR WITH HAZEL ON Saturday night. We got caught smoking weed in the parking lot by these two really hot guys, I'm talking so hot why are you talking to me kind of hot.

We shared our joint with them, and she and I secretly picked which guy we wanted. I took the taller one. He was wearing jeans, a white shirt, baseball hat, and he had dirty blonde hair, and brown eyes.

I guess I have a type.

Southern boys.

We stood out in the parking lot talking and it turns out they work on a farm; We got caught smoking weed by two cowboys.

After standing out there for about an hour or so we finally went inside and grabbed some food. We played a little pool, had some drinks, and decided to continue the party at their place.

Hazel and I were totally on the same page, and we hyped each other up on the drive there. It was a blast.

Going to strangers' places wasn't something neither of us did, like ever, so we sent our location to the other girls in the group chat to be safe.

Side note: I haven't talked about Hazel's story.

She had been with her boyfriend for four years when he suddenly left and moved away. He stopped talking to her and the rest of their friend circle, deleted his social media and erased himself from their lives completely… The group remained friends and moved on with their lives. It happened years ago, she said, and she's happier than she's ever been.

We drove up to a really cute place; it's a family-owned farm and they rent the house from their parents until they're ready to buy the whole thing.

They even grow their own weed! Yes, we got to try it and yes, it was awesome. The story is, Max's brother is the one who takes care of the plants, while Max handles the business side of things.

We paired up and spaced out a good bit, but close enough to pass a joint around.

Hazel and I tapped out right around the halfway mark, it was so strong. I was stoned and overly sensitive to my surroundings.

Hazel and her guy got handsy quickly, so they moved into the other room which made it awkward for a second. Max was sweet, asked me if I wanted to go swimming. I was down for it, so we went outside and stripped down to our underwear.

I traced my hand down his abs, I just had to touch them.

He laughed. I was stupid high.

I've noticed that when I'm high, I don't mask my feelings very well. I can also get really shy depending on who's around… and add the fact that this guy is totally and completely out of my league.

We're swimming and splashing each other around. He's being polite, like REALLY polite.

He asked me what I was thinking about, without thinking I said, "You". Next thing I knew, we were making out. We moved to the lawn chair for stability.

I straddled him, and he used his hands to squeeze my hips to rock us back and forth. He was hard and rubbing himself against me the whole time.

Neither one of us had a condom, our stuff was all inside.

Talk about a fucking mood killer.

We moved to his bedroom so we could be a little more comfortable. He locked the door behind us and turned some music on.

Pardon my french, but time slowed down and we just absolutely fucked the shit out of each other. It was a mixture of passionate and rough, leaning more towards rough.

He's also on the thicker side; I had to remind myself to breathe.

Things got messy; we were up against the wall at one point knocking shit all over the place. Now I get the reason for the music being so loud.

He was playing alternative metal or something, surprising for a cowboy, but it added to the sex rage we had going on, so I was into it.

By the time we finished up and found our way back to the living room, Hazel and his brother were wondering what happened to us, almost two hours had passed. I mean to be fair we did start out in the pool first, so.

We decided to exchange numbers and called it a night. Hazel and I shared stories on the way home and let's just say we both got some unexpected surprises tonight.

Sunday was a lazy day spent by the pool. The parents had some friends over, so I put in some headphones and kept to myself. Later, I took a bath and had whatever was leftover in the fridge for dinner.

I've been texting Max all day, he's sweet aside from the crazy sex we had.

He asked when we could hang out again and I wasn't sure what to tell him. I don't need to be wrapped up with another guy, but at the same time this is what guys do, they juggle girls for fun. So, if a guy can do it, then so can I… At least I know I'm safe about it.

He mentioned he was off next Saturday so we're going to get together then, and his brother and Hazel will be tagging along since they're digging each other.

Fast forward to Monday and Hazel and I have been talking a lot. She can't get over what happened this weekend either. Just crazy.

She and I told the rest of the girlfriend's group about these cowboy brothers, and they were so jealous, it was amusing.

I talked to Hunter a bit today, he's been busy with work taking on double shifts when he can. I did a little food shopping and some cleaning and that was about it for today. Might sit outside and do some reading.

Entry #40

WAS A TYPICAL WEEK: MORNING BIKE RIDES, AFTERNOON SWIMS, STEAMY showers; enjoying my free time. I texted Austin recently to check in, we haven't really spoken much since I swung by the office. He said he's just been busy with work and fixing go karts, but that was him pretty much blowing me off. Hopefully everything is okay…

Been texting with Max a good bit, well mostly at night because he's busy with work during the day.

No idea how old he is.

I saw Hunter on Wednesday but only to grab weed from him in between shifts. When the Fall semester kicks up, he won't be able to work as much, so I understand getting it all together now.

Hazel and I are hanging out with Max and his brother tomorrow, we're going to meet them at the beach around nine or so and go from there. She's a little nervous because she has actual feelings for Max's brother.

While I'm attracted to Max, I don't have feelings for him like that, so I told her I'd be her wing girl and not to worry about a thing.

Entry #41

LET'S TALK ABOUT SATURDAY.

Hazel and I met up with the guys at the beach around nine. We thought ahead so we practically had a picnic on the beach.

Around one or so, we decided to go back to their place. The guys lived an hour away, so Hazel and I had a little down time to talk on the way out there. She's super into Max's brother and she's going to go for it; I'm happy for her, she deserves to be happy.

She told me I should go for Max, but I told her I was doing me right now. Which is still true, granted I am tied up in crushing hard on Hunter.

Yeah, we had great sex and he's the perfect cowboy fantasy, but in the long run my mind was elsewhere.

We finally made it to the house and the guys were just jumping in the pool. We passed around a joint and before we knew it, we were stoned. Hazel and I got too high, so we got out and dried off, freshened up and felt way better.

We moved our party to the good ole living room and spread out on the couch. The other two had a blanket covering them so you know they weren't going to last long.

About halfway into the movie they did their walk of shame and headed out for some privacy. Max and I were chillin, just watching the movie when a sex scene came on.

I suddenly got nervous, maybe shy? I don't know. I never know what to do when a sex scene comes on tv and I'm watching it with someone.

He told me to come lay with him, so I did. He spooned me. I took my time getting comfortable and let's just say it didn't take long for him to catch on to what I was doing. He pulled me in tighter, reached into my shorts and started playing with my clit.

He told me not to make any noise, so we wouldn't get caught.

We weren't even covered up with a blanket or anything. Hazel and his brother could have walked out at any moment…

He was aggressive with me, and I enjoyed every minute of it. When I started to get loud, he covered my mouth for me. He asked me if I had had enough, he wanted to taste me.

I said, "Sure".

We changed up positions and let's just say my legs were weak by the time he was done with me.

We moved to his room and somehow my legs were on his shoulders within what felt like seconds after he locked the door.

Remember I said he was thick, so… watching him slide in and out of me drove me nuts.

Damn, I'm wet just writing about this.

Anyway. We switched it up a bit before we finished.

We sat on opposite facing sides of the bed as we got dressed. I cleaned myself up in the bathroom and came back to him lying on his bed. He packed a bowl for us.

I swear that weed has a mind of its own… Basically I was dazzled by the dick; I was high, and I knew what I wanted.

I climbed on top of him and raised his shirt off. We locked eyes as I moved my hands across his chest, and I told him how strong he felt.

He responded by calling me cute and said he didn't like being teased. Then he kissed my nose and smiled before he overpowered me and flipped me onto my stomach so he could assert his dominance. And indeed, he did. He told me I submit to him, not the other way around.

We found out the other two decided to go out for dinner, so we stayed behind and cooked whatever they had in the fridge.

Hazel and I drove together so I was pretty much stuck until she got back. Not that I was really feeling stuck, Max is cool and all, I'm just not trying to stick around any longer than I have to.

We laid out on the lawn chairs and caught the sunset. Hazel and his brother finally got back, so we decided to wrap it up and head out for the evening. It had been a very long day and I needed a shower.

Hazel said she and Max's brother are officially a thing, and dinner tonight was their first date. Happy for her, most definitely! But I hope hanging out doesn't get weird, I can't be there every time she wants to hang out with him.

Max is sweet and incredibly hot, but I don't need to be around him that much, I'm not trying to get myself into anymore boy trouble than I'm already in.

I am going to establish some boundaries with him though, and I need to be honest with him.

Hunter texted me that he's off work tomorrow night and wanted to know if I wanted to swing by his place… I haven't seen him much, so I obviously didn't hesitate to respond.

...

I realize I haven't done much self-reflection lately.

Looking back on how this summer has been going, I still can't believe what's happened, I'm finally out here doing things and having fun.

While I wish the summer had a little more time left in it, I am excited to get back to a work environment. More importantly I'm excited to replenish my finances.

I will add that I'm proud for putting myself out there and not holding back. I'm enjoying this new me and truthfully, I wish I let her out a long time ago.

Entry #42

JUST ANOTHER RAINY DAY; I STAYED IN AND CAUGHT UP ON THIS BOOK I'VE been reading.

It's been a while since I've sat and read for hours on end; hell, I even kept my phone on silent and pretty much didn't look at it again until it was time for me to head to Hunters.

I got myself together and went for a cute, relaxed look. His roommate was gone for the night, so he and I were alone.

He was already in the kitchen when I got there, and had a joint rolled for us.

About an hour in we're both stoned, and dinner's just about ready. We sat down at the table and ate for what felt like a really long time. It's not even like we talked about anything in particular, we just had a good conversation, and it went wherever it went.

We moved to the couch and relit the joint. I developed the major giggles so that was embarrassing… Thankfully they didn't last long, and he got a kick out of it.

Once I got myself under control, he put a movie on and without hesitating we cozied right up next to each other like we've always been doing that. I mean sometimes we do, sometimes we don't.

Of all movies, he puts on a scary one. Now I'm all for a good scary movie, but a comedy must follow so I don't have bad dreams. We were also high, so I didn't see how that was a smart movie choice.

<u>I grabbed his arm every time something scared me.</u>

And I was scared a lot...

I didn't catch this until halfway through the movie, he didn't say anything about it either.

The movie ended and I told him he owed me a hug to make me feel better after watching a scary movie. He told me to climb on over and I could hug him all I wanted. So, I did.

After I hugged him, I pulled away and we looked at each other for a second. He took his shirt off, so I took off mine. He relaxed his arms behind his head. I traced my finger all across his chest and up and down his arms, I even played with his hair. He pulled me in close by the middle part of my bra, so close our noses were touching.

I could tell he wanted to say something but was holding back. I nudged my way in for a kiss.

We made out like teenagers, it was hot, but also it felt like it meant something, maybe. We took our clothes off and finished with me bent over the edge of the couch. We wrapped up this time.

I excused myself to straighten up in the bathroom and no sooner after that I went home, not to mention he had work in the morning and it was getting kind of late. I did get some leftovers to take home with me.

...

I showered and now here I am. I couldn't get here fast enough.

I've decided I'm going to be honest with Max the next time I see him and make sure that we're on the same page. I also don't think I should really sleep with him again. Austin and I are chill as far as I know… we'll be working together soon anyway.

As far as Hunter goes, he and I have been honest about everything from the very beginning.

After all, we both kind of did admit our mutual attraction to each other, but attraction doesn't always equate to feelings.

And it doesn't appear that either of us are going to bring it up anytime soon… we haven't even talked about the fact that we broke one of our rules.

I'm just going to spend the rest of the summer having fun, doing me, and overall, just going with the flow. Whatever happens, happens. My first day of job shadowing is on September 2nd and that's not too far away. That's what I should mainly be focused on right now, anyway.

Entry #43

SATURDAY AUGUST 17TH 2013

I SAW MAX LAST NIGHT AND I TOLD HIM I WANTED TO BE HONEST WITH HIM IN that I wasn't looking for a relationship or anything serious. He was super chill about it because he doesn't want anything serious either, he seemed relieved that I felt the same.

Ouch.

I'm glad we got that out of the way, I do feel better now.

Hazel was out with his brother, so it was just he and I at the house. We passed a bottle of whiskey back and forth until the alcohol did its magic. We decided to go night swimming, only this time naked.

Both of us were smashed, he had whiskey dick. Hazel and his brother got back just in time… I really needed to go home.

We grabbed some food on our way, and she dropped me off at my place. The food helped a little bit, but I was still plastered. I struggled, but I managed to take a shower. Made it to the bed and passed out.

I woke up this morning less hungover than I expected, so that was nice.

Had a decent breakfast and once I felt hydrated, went out and sat by the pool. The parents were out there planting flowers and making the place look pretty.

We talked a little, had some lunch and spent the rest of the afternoon together. They told me they never see me anymore and they miss me, but they're glad I'm having fun and doing well.

Shoot, if only they knew the things I was up to.

I miss them too, but I'm enjoying my summer more.

Yes, I'll admit, I've changed, but I feel pretty fucking great right now, so I'm going to enjoy this high for as long as I can.

I stayed for dinner and went back to my place after to shower. I got out and had a missed call from Scarlett. I was kind of nervous to call her back; we haven't really spoken, like she wasn't responding to any calls or texts, so I was just surprised to hear from her, I guess.

I called her back, before I could even get a word in, she told me she wanted to come down and visit and she wanted to know if Monday was too soon. I was a little surprised but also excited, of course I told her to come down.

I had no idea what we would do, but I knew we would figure something out.

$\mathcal{E}$ntry #44

I WOKE UP AROUND NINE AND HAD SOME COFFEE OUT ON THE BALCONY, wasn't really feeling breakfast, the parents wanted to go out, but I wanted to stay in.

I didn't have a whole lot of cleaning to do, but enough before I had someone spend a few days here. I took an edible, turned on some music and got to cleaning.

I didn't really feel the edible, so I started smoking and that's when I really felt it.

I cleaned for about two hours when I decided to make some lunch. I had some chicken in the fridge, so I went ahead and grilled some for a salad.

Out of nowhere, my confidence peaked, I was feeling good about myself, so I cleaned the rest of the place in my underwear. I only had laundry left so it wasn't like I was breaking a sweat or anything.

I finished up laundry and lounged around for the remainder of the evening, ordered pizza for dinner, and took some nudes to kill the time. I had them throw extra parmesan on the pizza this time; can't wait to smell that perfection.

Around nine/nine-thirty Hunter texted me and after a few minutes of boring work talk I sent him one of the pictures, he called me a few minutes later after he finished up work.

I was thinking about pizza not sex, but I played along with his dirty conversation until he got here. He didn't even go home to shower first; he came straight here, with the classic burnt kitchen grease and sweat smell of his.

I was still in my underwear when he showed up, I threw on a robe to answer the door. He walked inside and took forever to settle in.

He sat down on a chair and pulled me along with him. He dragged his lips across my chest, then up and down my neck.

I was holding on by his shoulders, and he was rubbing me over my underwear. Our bodies were pressed up against each other and his eyes locked with mine.

It was really, fucking hot. I was about to cum when the fucking pizza guy showed up.

He answered the door and told me we'd resume our fun later.

Tease.

Over pizza, I told him about Scarlett coming to visit before deciding on a movie. We rolled a joint and the next thing we knew, it was one in the morning.

Both of us were tired, I told him he could stay if he wanted to, and he did. I went to my bathroom to freshen up, he in the other, and we met back in bed. Didn't even have sex… he fell right to sleep and I'm here writing.

Talk about a fantasy come true.

Usually, he's pretty clean shaven but he's got a little five o'clock shadow coming in and I wish he would grow it out, he would look so good with a beard. Maybe he'll grow it out in the winter.

It's weird looking over my shoulder and there's a man asleep in my bed.

Well, maybe weird isn't the right word. I guess I don't know how to pinpoint how it makes me feel, because it makes me feel a lot of different things. All good things, just a little confusing also you could say.

Tell you what though, he looks sexy when he's sleeping.

Entry #45

THURSDAY AUGUST 22ND 2013

HUNTER WOKE UP BEFORE ME, I HEARD HIM IN THE SHOWER. I THOUGHT ABOUT joining him, but I was so comfortable, still a little tired anyway, so I stayed in bed.

He came out with just a towel on and obviously one thing led to another. He told me he had to make up for falling asleep on me last night. What I was fawning over more was the fact that he let himself into my shower while I was sleeping.

While I was curious about what he used in there, I didn't want to obsess about what any of it could or could not mean. Trying not to, at least..

I made us some coffee and we drank it in the kitchen. I was sitting on the counter in my robe, and he was standing on the opposite side, shirtless in his shorts, talking about the day ahead.

He had to be at work at two and was in no rush to get there so we hung out and cooked some breakfast together. Well, he cooked, and I stayed where I was, sipping on my coffee.

He didn't want any help and he didn't even ask me to move, he moved around me instead.

I love watching him cook.

You can tell how much cooking makes him happy, and I like that he shares it with me.

We ate outside, it was beautiful outside so why not. Granted the parents were already at work, I know they saw his jeep again. Only a matter of time before they accidentally run into each other if were not careful.

Hunter mentioned he and his friends are all getting together on the boat to close out the end of the summer with a party at the end of the month. The girlfriends told me about it earlier in the week and already invited me, but Hunter was inviting me to go <u>with him</u>.

He's picking me up so we can drive together, I was instructed to pack an overnight bag just in case.

I was excited, but I needed to figure out what to wear.

A few hours later Scarlett arrived, I couldn't believe she drove. She arrived Monday a little after four, took a short nap, and we spent the remaining sunlight out by the pool.

I could tell she was hiding something. We hadn't spoken for almost an entire month when she randomly called me to come down and visit.

We had Chinese delivered for dinner and no sooner called it a night. I stayed up and read, Scarlett slept on her air mattress.

We woke up around eight the next morning and got ready to head to the beach. Later we met up with Hazel and the other girlfriends for drinks at some bar.

I was excited for Scarlett to meet everyone; I was really looking forward to showing her the life I'm building down here. Truthfully, I'm having a blast and I want her to know all about it. She's never held back from sharing, so I'm excited to be in the spotlight this time.

We met up with the others around six for drinks and apps. We had a blast… stayed out until eleven or so.

Wednesday rained all fucking day unfortunately, but it was for the best because we were both sunburnt as fuck, and really didn't need any more sun.

We hit up the store and got supplies so we could day drink and watch movies all day… and that is exactly what we did. We got drunk and spilled secrets.

I didn't give her the full secret, but I told her how Hunter and I have been spending more time together. Kept the sleepovers to myself.

Not entirely sure why I decided to hide that.

I did finally tell her about Max… I <u>had</u> to brag about the sexy weed growing cowboy.

…

So, Scarlett spilled on what's been going on; she lost her job and she's looking for a new one. That explained the sudden trip down here. She wouldn't tell me what happened, I wondered if it had anything to do with why I haven't heard from her in a while.

She still had the same phone number and the same cell phone, same car… so I don't know.

This was the first time I realized we were both keeping secrets. I'm not mad, our friendship has obviously changed, I just can't help but wonder where we go from here.

She got serious for a minute and asked me how I was doing here… I was honest with her.

I told her about the job shadowing, the group chats, and then I bragged about where I get to live.

I hope I didn't hurt her, but I'm much happier here and I'm not going to lie about it. Obviously, I reminded her that I missed her and stuff, but it was about me in that moment, so I took it.

She told me that she told Benji she was coming down to see me. I hadn't thought of him in a while.

I quickly reminded myself that I'm no longer living in the past... we had our goodbye and moved on. I don't know why she had to bring him up and I was a little annoyed about it. He and I will always be friends, I just didn't think it was necessary to tell him she was coming to see me, let alone tell me about it.

Made me wonder for a second how close they were, but what's that going to do for me? Noda damn thing.

We watched high school dramas, chick flicks, ate dinner, and eventually sobered up. We did go to bed early because she had some driving ahead of her. Probably wasn't the best idea to drink the day before driving home, but she seemed fine.

I told her she could have stayed a little longer, but she wanted to get home so she could find a new job. I understood that.

We went out for breakfast pretty early and she left from there. It was a sad goodbye, I really miss her, but something just felt off the entire time.

There's something going on that she's not telling me. Mines a sex secret, means nothing to her, but whatever she's hiding, has to be good.

I hope things get better. I really do, I mean we've known each other for a very long time, and nothing has come between us before, so what could it be now?

After breakfast I went home and pulled off a three-hour bike ride. The weather was perfect, and I had music; nothing else mattered.

I got back and made a grilled chicken sandwich for lunch. Noticed I was low on groceries, so I did a little food shopping after and ran into Max. We did our shopping together then parted ways; we haven't talked a whole lot since we got plastered together. It was interesting to see the public side of him since we're usually by ourselves.

Side note: I still needed an outfit for the boat party, so Hazel and I decided on a shopping trip for tomorrow.

I spent the rest of my Thursday relaxing, cooked myself a nice dinner and read a little. Even checked out my flash cards… almost time to get to work.

Mom has no idea I've been studying by the way.

Entry #46

HAZEL AND I HAD THE BEST DAY SHOPPING.

We met up at the mall around noon, legit went to six different stores and managed to sneak in some lunch and a few drinks.

Okay, hear me out. I bought a jumpsuit for the boat party. It's primarily navy blue, with thin white vertical stripes. It has a V-neckline, and you can definitely see some side boob. Even better, when Hunter takes it off me, I'll be completely naked underneath.

Hello one-piece easy access for the win.

I paired it with some wedges and a thin extra-long necklace; it'll cover the boobs just right. Hazel's outfit is dope too, she's excited. We left the mall and went our separate ways; she's going to her boyfriend's house tonight. Max invited me over, but I wasn't feeling it.

Period started, but it's probably for the best anyway.

I hung around and tried on everything I just bought. I texted Max a little until he stopped responding.

Hazel told me he didn't have a girl over. I'm not stressed, I've been doing other things myself.

I was feeling super indecisive about dinner, so I decided on pancakes. I spent the next three hours watching tv when I got a text from Hunter that he was close to getting off work and was wondering what I was up to.

I was honest about my inability to have sex tonight, and he was still cool to come over. He shows up and comes right up to lay with me on the couch. He grabbed my boobs and told me he had a rough day and needed to feel some titties.

When passing the joint back and forth, he said I smelled like pancakes, I told him I had some for dinner. He hadn't eaten yet, so we whipped some up really quick.

We talked about his final semester coming up and how he's ready to graduate... He's going to be busy until then. He asked me about the job shadowing and while it's only for two weeks, it has the potential to turn into a job, so my schedule will be different, too.

We reminisced on the beauty of summer and once again completely ignored the fact that we had spent so much of it together.

I could have brought it up, but I'm learning that living in the moment is what's important, not constantly wanting to label things. I also don't want to jinx anything because this could literally be a summer fling for all I know, and here I am getting all worked up about it. So, yeah. It was nice to hang out and enjoy each other's company.

We watched about two more episodes of this cooking show before he headed out; he's working a double shift tomorrow and needed sleep. We're spoiled living so close to each other, I think that's why we hang out so much. Plus, it's nice to not have to drive so far to pick up weed.

Tomorrow begins the final seven days of summer. Cheers to having the best time ever!

Entry #47

SATURDAY AUGUST 24TH 2013

FUCK, I FORGOT ABOUT MY BIRTHDAY.

My fucking 25th is next Friday and I completely forgot. Usually, Scarlett and I plan something with the rest of the group but obviously that's not going to happen this year.

I suddenly found myself super homesick. Yes, I am building a pretty sweet life down here, but that doesn't mean I can't miss the old one sometimes.

I was scrolling through social media and saw a picture of Benji at his parent's restaurant. I started to feel feelings.

I almost texted him but that's only because I know he knows I saw Scarlett, and I'm sure she's not holding back any details.

I needed to clear my head, so I went for a bike ride, I put in ten miles without even realizing I had gone that far… I guess I really needed it. I showered and finished up with a vitamin c face mask and a frozen pizza for lunch.

Remember the wives group chat? They still exist and we still talk from time to time, everyone has their own shit going on with summer coming to an end. They invited me to go out with them tonight, so I decided to go for it.

We met up at this rooftop bar with live music, it was probably the fanciest place I have been to since moving down here.

We caught up and had a decent night together; it was a good time. Their husbands started showing up which only meant that Austin was nearby, and we hadn't seen each other since I basically rejected him at the office. He also hasn't seen me dressed this slutty before.

I blame my period and the alcohol. And his lips. We made out in the basement bathroom; it was squeaky clean though, I'm no whore.

He picked me up and sat me on the counter. I wrapped my legs tightly around him and we sucked face.

We weren't even having sex and he still managed to land me in one of the craziest situations I've been in.

Maybe once or twice, I have fantasized about what he would do to me if he had the chance.

We're lucky we didn't get caught. We found our way back to the group and about an hour later I went home. Watching married people grind on each other in public is not my kind of vibe at this moment in life.

I went home and I got really high. I'm so stoned I'm surprised I wrote for this long; I mean I biked ten fucking miles, I'm feeling a bit exhausted now that I'm sitting still.

I don't know what the fuck to do about my birthday this year, I really don't think I'm feeling up for anything. Plus, how do I even tell people without looking like I'm looking for attention?

Also, why the fuck did I give in to Austin when I have it so good with Hunter? Hunter suggested breaking the rules first. And while I think Austin and I both disregarded our boundaries tonight, I'm still the common denominator.

I've noticed having fun and living in the moment has consequences.

Entry #48

I WANT TO TALK ABOUT THE VIEW RIGHT NOW. THERE'S LIGHT THUNDER IN THE background, rumbling around me. The sun is barely peeking through the clouds, so the grass appears a darker shade of green. It's raining at a soothing pace.

Birds are chirping and frogs are making the ribbit noise they make. I really can't get over the thunder though. If you really sit and listen to it, it's almost like you're catching a wave and floating along. Nature's lullaby.

As you can tell, I've been stoned pretty much all day, it's been nice to unwind and relax entirely.

I gave in and talked to Hazel about my birthday, of course she wanted to throw a party. I suggested we just toast since we'll all be together at the boat party anyway. She wasn't convinced easily, but that's what we're going to do. And she told me not to worry about anything, so that was nice.

Just one thought I need to work out.

Potential guest list…

Hazel is a part of the girlfriend's group so obviously all of them plus their guys would be there, including Hunter. Hazel's dating Max's brother, so Max may want to tag along.

Max and I have established boundaries and are both on the same page, but that doesn't mean I would be cool with him and Hunter running into each other.

And then there's the wives' group and Austin, who she doesn't know a whole lot about, at least I don't think so, I mean it may have come up in conversation before.

Anyway, if I play my cards right, maybe Max won't be able to make it. But if he does, what do I do if they run into each other? I already told Hunter I was going with him to the party.

I don't know what to think; but my head's running every possible scenario right now. Too much to keep up with.

I decided to agree to let Hazel handle everything which in turn also transfers the stress to her, so I'm just going to do my best to sit back and relax. Fingers crossed.

It rained all fucking day so there wasn't much to do, thankfully the forecast is looking a little more favorable over the next few days.

I decided to do a massive, big cleaning; not like I have much to do but I got deep into it. Like I dusted ceiling fans, scrubbed the tubs and the shower, cleaned out the fridge and the microwave, mopped- like really mopped, washed my bedding; Yeah, I did a lot.

Wasn't until about seven when I realized the time. After heavy cleaning I wasn't really feeling up to cooking, so I went ahead and ordered a pizza. ETA was eight forty-five, so I went ahead and took a hot shower. I love steam; I should really check out a sauna.

Pizza finally showed, I just ate it out of the box on the couch; I was really high by the time it got here, I was prepping for it. Tasted amazing; the crust was so crunchy.

Even after crushing the pie, I was still high. I texted my weed expert and asked him what was up… basically I should have allowed more time for the weed to kick in because it's a creeper strain, and it sneaks up on ya.

Whoops.

He had just gotten out of the shower and into bed after working all day otherwise he would have come by, so… we talked on the phone instead.

He wanted to get on my level, so he packed a bowl or two and once he was where he wanted to be, he brought out this weed game he's got, it's like a conversation starter.

Mostly hypothetical questions, but some of them were asking about who we are and what kind of things we like.

One of the questions just so happened to ask what our birthday month was, so of course that lead to him finding out my birthday is on Friday.

He asked me what the plans were, and I told him about Hazel planning a toast for me Saturday night. He asked me about Friday, my actual birthday, and I honestly hadn't thought about it. So that's what I told him. He said he had to work but could swing by after if I was up for it.

We moved on with the conversation without confirming plans, he could tell I was stressed… he asked me what I was thinking about. He's got a habit of doing that.

I told him I was stressed about my birthday.

Which wasn't a lie.

And like the gentleman he is, he did everything he could to comfort me with that Southern charm of his.

He then eventually charmed me into phone sex once he knew I was feeling better.

Entry #49

I RANDOMLY WOKE UP AROUND SIX THIS MORNING AND COULDN'T FALL BACK to sleep. It wasn't raining out, so I decided to go for a walk on the beach; I don't normally get up that early, so I decided to take advantage given I'm about an hour drive away.

I didn't exactly make it in time, but I still managed to see a killer view of the sun rise. I got lost in the ocean views and noticed three hours had passed.

Not to mention I was getting a little hungry, so I made my way back to the car and stopped by a cute little place for breakfast on my way home. Made me consider that I should start dining out more often instead of ordering delivery.

After breakfast I headed home and showered. Hazel had the day off, so she came by around one, and we did some light day drinking planning my birthday toast.

We talked about the guest list and when she asked about inviting anyone else, I decided not to bring up Austin and the wives. Things were confusing with him as is.

If any of them find out which I'm sure they'll see on social media, I'll just tell them my friends toasted me after finding out about my birthday the day after.

Now, I kind of ditched Max the last time he wanted to hang out, and the time before that we got drunk and went skinny dipping... now that he knows it's my birthday, I can't let myself be alone with him, it's as plain and simple as that.

NOT TO MENTION, I'M GOING TO THE PARTY WITH HUNTER. HE'S LITERALLY DRIVING ME.

I may be stressing all of this for nothing. I mean technically I'm not dating any of these guys and I've been honest with each of them. I just don't want to ruin what fun I have going on, ya know?

To be brutally honest, none of them have asked me if I was seeing anyone else, so it's not like I'm lying or hiding anything. I mean shit same for them, I could be a random booty call for all I know.

So honestly, fuck it. Back to my birthday plans.

Decided on nothing fancy, just getting champagne and a few extra party favors.

I considered returning the jumpsuit I bought, but I think it will work. The only difference in the night is the toast, so, it's really not that big of a deal.

Tomorrow I'll do my food shopping, and Wednesday I'll go shopping for some new work outfits; it's causal work attire and nothing I have really works for that.

Hazel and I drunkenly ordered burgers. We ate and sobered up enough for her to head home. I spent the rest of the evening catching up on some reading and writing out here on the balcony- it's been peaceful.

I talked to Scarlett a little bit today, she brought up my birthday and I told her what was going on, she seemed happy for me, but I wonder if she was feeling the same way I was.

Made me think about Benji a little; granted it was the first birthday apart with us being broken up, now we're not even in the same state so even if we did want to see each other, we couldn't.

Feels… weird?

I know… it sounds crazy.

I just need to get through the first and then it won't feel so weird after that.

Time heals.

It's been a long day; I'm going to call it a night.

Entry #50

TODAY WASN'T TOO EVENTFUL; WENT ON A TWO-HOUR BIKE RIDE THIS MORNING and made out well at the grocery store after.

Decided to plan a menu and meal prep for next week since I'll be pulling a 9-5 schedule for the first time in a while.

I cut up vegetables, chicken, steak, some pork and even portioned out some ground beef; I was busy for what felt like hours.

Max texted me a little after work and told me he's looking forward to Saturday night; I wasn't sure how he meant that, so I continued with the conversation and eventually changed the subject. It was time to figure out dinner, so I believe I left him on read at that point.

I decided to keep it small and made some tacos, after all it is Tuesday so why not do a simple taco Tuesday. After dinner, I threw on a face and eye mask and soaked away in the tub chillin to some music.

Hunter called me, he wanted to join, I told him he was interrupting my self-care time, but he said he would make it worth it if I let him swing by.

My curiosity got the best of me so I told him he could come by, giving me enough time to unlock the door and finish my masks.

He got in some Pineapple Express, so he rolled a fat joint for us. Of course, we had to enjoy that in the tub, so I added some more bubbles, and we passed it back and forth until it felt a little claustrophobic.

We moved into the shower and that just intensified my high, not sure how he felt, but he did get handsy. I reciprocated. Fooling around in the shower incredibly high was a little tricky, but we made it work.

He fingered me and I gave him head. As much as we wanted to have sex right there, we knew it was better to wait for the bed. We washed our bodies and got the hell out of there. Barely had time to dry off before my legs were over his shoulders and he was plowing right into me.

Pineapple Express is good for the sex drive, and I hope he has a lot of it, because I like it and I want more of it.

We got dressed and moved the conversation to the kitchen so we could hydrate. We chatted about this weekend; I told him not to worry about it, but he insisted we do something when he gets home from work Friday night.

He's going to pick me up around ten-thirty, so he has time to shower and clean up. He won't tell me what we're doing.

Entry #51

TODAY WAS A SHOP TILL YOU DROP KIND OF DAY!

Started my morning with another two-hour bike ride, took a dip in the pool after, then showered. Made myself some coffee, a nice breakfast and finally headed out to go shopping.

I needed at least three outfits… two for work, and one for birthday evening with Hunter. It was hard to shop for a night I knew nothing about, but I made out well.

For work, I bought these olive-green pants with a cute ribbon for the belt, and a solid black sleeveless shirt to go with it. Paired with some nude heels I have in my closet.

The other outfit is a cute pair of light blue pants, a white blouse, and a black blazer I'll probably roll the sleeves up, and pair with some black heels I have in my closet.

Sneaky sexy, yet still appropriate for work.

Lastly, for the afterhours birthday evening, I played it cute. I went with a long sleeve romper, it's a dusty rose pinkish color with gold polka dots scattered all over. I'll pair this with white shoes in case we do any walking.

I did some really great work today. I'm going to look incredible and I'm so damn excited.

Of course, I tried everything on again once I got home, but this time as the complete set - shoes, jewelry, and all.

I snapped a picture of myself in each look. Seeing myself like this… it's such a fucking high, I don't know how else to explain it.

I've come such a long way and it feels good to be where I'm at. Moving down here was a great decision and I'm glad I made the move… I'm learning things about myself.

Entry #52

TODAY WAS A GREAT FUCKING DAY.

I woke up and made some muffins for breakfast, with some coffee and bacon on the side.

Around lunch time I went and got a ninety-minute full body massage; totally melted into the table, it was so relaxing. I then went home and took a nice long bath, almost fell asleep in the tub.

I took a cool shower after to wake myself back up and spent the rest of the day reading and finalizing my spa appointments for tomorrow.

Every year on the day before my birthday I like to eat a nice dinner with exactly two bottles of wine. One for drinking while you're cooking with a splash or two for the meal, and one for the dinner table.

I was a bottle in and just sitting down to eat when Benji called, he knows it's my thing… after all his grandma is the one who got me into doing it. She told me her birthday secret was to treat herself the day before her actual birthday, because "you deserve to celebrate yourself privately".

While we didn't cook the exact same meal, they were both coincidentally ready, so we went ahead and ate dinner together on the phone. While slightly uncomfortable, it was kind of nice, and I feel like we got a little closure we didn't know we needed.

We stayed on the phone through dessert and after dinner clean up; just chatted away about the summer and how the restaurant is going and such. We mostly talked about him; it was nice to hear how well he's doing.

My phone was hot we had been talking for so long.

We finished the second bottle of wine together and put the phone on speaker while we got ourselves ready for bed.

We talked each other's ears off all the way up until midnight so he could be the first to wish me a happy birthday. This one poked my heart for a moment before I snapped back to reality.

We soon hung up and I've been writing in here since.

I can't believe I'm twenty-five.

So much shit has already happened to me... But also, some really great things too, and I realize now that if they didn't happen the way they did, I wouldn't be who or where I am today.

I could sit here and play the what if game all day long if I wanted, but at the end of the day I can finally say that I'm happy where I am, and I truly think I'm heading in the right direction. I've battled a lot of obstacles and I deserve to have some positivity.

Whether I continue to be single or find my way into a relationship this next chapter of my life, I promise to always continue to take care of myself and my needs.

I promise to be honest with myself about how I'm feeling and what I truly desire; regardless of how that looks.

I'm enjoying this new and free version of myself, and I want to hang onto it for as long as possible.

These upcoming years are the ones that matter most. Things sure do look different now than when they did at eighteen, even twenty. I feel like I have some catching up to do in life and I do believe change can be good if you can find yourself a way to welcome it. I'm excited to see what this next year brings me!

Entry #53

I WOKE UP AND HAD COFFEE AND BREAKFAST AT THIS CHIC RUSTIC PLACE downtown. It had a beautiful view of the cobblestone streets and the old rustic storefronts, wrapped in vine and all.

I got a blowout and my hair stayed intact, a manicure with a hand massage, and a pedicure with a hot stone foot massage.

I stayed downtown and grabbed lunch at this local seafood restaurant with the parents, had a bright and shiny view of the water…. Reminded them how thankful I was to have been given the opportunity to come down here with them. I appreciate it more than they realize.

They surprised me with a gift card to a local boutique, so I did a little shopping when they went back to work and got myself a new bag. It's a backpack, so we'll see how I like it (trying something new here).

About an hour later Mom texted me asking when I would be home because she had another surprise me for. Considering how well the day was already going, I was feeling hopeful I was in for something nice.

I got home and noticed some cars in the driveway that I didn't recognize… they had South Carolina plates, so it was either someone local or rental cars.

I had no idea what I was going to be walking into. I panicked.

I walked in the door and heard, "surprise!" The crowd consisted of the parents, some of their coworkers, some of the wives' and their husbands, and then Austin.

Apparently, Mom told him it was my birthday and she asked for some help with the guest list… While I was surprised to see everyone here for me, I couldn't believe who all showed up, especially at six on a Friday night. Such a random time.

Got to give it to the parents for the surprise. I mean we just had lunch together and it didn't come up… did they even have to work today, or did they take the day off to do this just for me? I was surprised yes, but I was more appreciative of what they did.

There was food, drinks, decorations, and a cake… It was so sweet of them to do this for me. What I was really panicking about was the fact that Austin was there, and Hunter was picking me up after work tonight.

All the "what if's" raced through my mind. And then I realized I should probably walk in the door and say hello to everyone.

Of course, I started with the parents. They told me they didn't want me to feel alone on my birthday since we're new to the area.

Little did they know, I had plans later that night.

I couldn't tell them what I was nervous about, so I thanked them, and they re-introduced me to their coworkers before I moved on to Austin and his friends.

Mind you, while I had my hair and nails done, I wasn't exactly looking very glamourous. I was in sweatpants and a tank top, so basically my boobs were on display. I was saving the real birthday outfit for tonight with Hunter.

I thanked everyone and we chatted for a minute. Austin told me to come look at something in the kitchen, of course I followed, he helped my mom plan a surprise birthday party for me…

Dude. He got me flowers and a card; it was SO sweet. We were alone in the kitchen so he gave me a kiss on the cheek.

I wasn't sure how to respond. I gave him a hug and thanked him for everything.

While I screamed in my head, he had to be gone by ten.

We made ourselves a drink and went outside where everyone migrated to now that I was home. That's where all the food was anyway.

Eight o'clock rolled in and people started to head out to get to their kids and pets… Again, the party was an awesome surprise and I feel truly blessed to have cool people by my side, but I needed everyone gone.

Eventually I was alone with Austin out by the pool. We rolled up our pants and stuck our feet in the water. Even the parents went inside so I could "enjoy the rest of my birthday evening" per Mom.

I swear, she's trying to set me up with Austin or something. She knows it's Hunter's jeep that's here all the time, so what's her deal? I thought we squashed this.

I had bigger problems at that moment. It was a little after nine and Austin was still there.

He asked me what I had going on for the rest of the night… I was honest and said I had plans tonight. He asked me if it was with the person Mom asked him about. I was like, "Wait, what"?

When she asked him about a guest list, she asked if he knew anything about Hunters jeep. Apparently, she brought up how she'd seen it parked overnight and was wondering who it was so they could have been invited.

SHE KNOWS WHO IT IS.

I nearly threw up.

I wasn't lying when I said I had friends over. But I did fib. Since he doesn't know Hazel at this moment in time, I told him we would get too drunk sometimes and she'd have to spend the night.

He and I aren't dating so I didn't owe him an explanation, but I do generally care about him as a friend, and I didn't want to jeopardize that by making things any more complicated than they already were.

He seemed to understand, but I'm sure he's a little extra curious now. I mean I would be if I were him.

He was polite and asked me when I needed to be ready by and I told him ten. He took the hint, I felt kind of bad, but I didn't know about the surprise party, and I already had plans. After all I did hang out with him for most of the night, so there's that.

I walked him to his car and thanked him again for the flowers and for helping out with everything, it was nice to see everyone, and I appreciated them thinking of me. He told me everyone adores me and is here for me anytime. I didn't expect that honestly, I haven't known them for very long, so that made me feel happy.

I was in awe of what he said. He hugged me goodnight and as he was leaving, he told me he looked forward to seeing me bright and early Monday morning.

I gave him a friendly heads up that I'm not always a morning person and he said before driving off, "Even better".

Like, what the fuck was that supposed to mean?

I didn't have a lot of time to get ready, so I had to move fast.

I took a mini shower and washed the essentials. Thankfully my hair was still decent looking by the end of all that. I got all dressed up and ready to go.

Hunter showed up at exactly ten-thirty and met me by my door. He blindfolded me as he walked me to the jeep, assuring me I was safe and that he wasn't on his way to dump my body.

Wasn't sure why he had to blindfold me on the walk instead of after I got in, but I was totally digging the suspense, so I went along with it.

We played a round of mini golf and finished up with some cosmic bowling that lasted until a little after midnight. I bet he was tired, he worked like ten hours on his feet all day.

I may have been a bit tipsy on the drive home, which also meant I had the giggles… we smoked during mini golf and had drinks while we bowled. He only had two drinks, so he was fine, I on the other hand had gotten a head start at my surprise party so I was feeling good vibes all night.

I must have thanked him like five times for taking me out. He went out of his way, and I told him he didn't have to do that.

He knew I was feeling a little homesick, so he wanted to make sure I had a good time.

I told him how much that meant to me and then we pulled up to my house.

He turned the jeep off and we unbuckled our seat belts. I invited him inside, he followed.

I leaned against the kitchen table, and we watched each other take our shoes off.

He walked up to me and put his forehead against mine.

Who knew a pair of eyes could make you feel so at home.

He responded in all seriousness with, "I want you".

I said, "You already have me".

We both got quiet… still locked in on each other's eyes. He told me he hasn't been honest with me. My heart temporarily sank as I waited for him to confess what it was he had to say. He developed feelings for me, but he didn't want to say anything because he knew how important it was to me to establish myself and find my way after moving to a new place.

He was respecting my wishes…

I mean when he took me to the treehouse for the first time, we both admitted our attraction to the other. I guess I just didn't hold onto that as much as he did.

Here I was trying to keep my feelings in check when we've wanted the same thing this entire time. But he's right, I was serious when I said I wanted to focus on myself.

I told him I enjoyed who we are together and was worried that labeling it would ruin it. I reminded him of the changes we have coming up in our lives with school and work, our future careers… but he didn't flinch, he said we would work around it. He promised being together would be a power move, not a distraction. He was so confident we would be okay, so I believed him.

We finally broke eye contact when we kissed.

I wrapped my legs around him, and he carried me over to the bed and laid me down. One hand held him up over me, and the other brushed the hair off my face. He told me I was beautiful and hoped I had a nice birthday.

That was the first time he called me beautiful.

Though it was after midnight, we had our birthday fun, and then we had sex together for the first time as boyfriend and girlfriend. I'm excited to find out what new girlfriend perks I have to look forward to; we already do so much together.

He finally dosed off about ten minutes ago and here I am at four fifty-eight in the morning, writing it all down before I forget… because let me tell you, today has been a fucking day!!

I've got to get to bed. Tomorrow, today, is the last day of the summer boat party and I want to be well rested for that… Considering we'll be shocking everyone with the news that we're together.

And Max is going to be there, and Hazel doesn't know that Hunter and I have been hanging out for as long as we have.

While I'm sure it's exhaustion and anxiety, I hope things don't get weird. I mean I haven't seen Max in a while and Hazel will be too happy for me to ask me any questions, so it'll be what it is.

Fuck. I hope I'm this confident in the morning.

Entry # 54

SOMETIMES YOU JUST NEED TO GET RIGHT TO IT.

Hunter woke up early, I think around eight and he took a shower. I was not ready to get out of bed yet. He came back to lay with me, and I fell back to sleep.

Around ten or so I woke up, for real that time, and he was in the kitchen making breakfast. He found the fruit in the freezer and made us strawberry and blueberry pancakes, eggs, and bacon.

Must be one of the girlfriend perks I've unlocked.

We ate outside on the balcony. Didn't even care if the parents were home or not, they weren't outside so that was cool with me. Not that I'm hiding him, I just don't want to have that conversation with them right now.

I cleaned up breakfast and he whipped up a batch of special cookies for the party. He made cannabutter earlier in the week.

Since I'm dating my weed dealer now, does that make me a stoner queen?

The cookies were strong, thank God we split one… We fell asleep for almost three hours.

Woke up and realized we needed to get ready, he headed back to his place, and I worked on myself here.

When he came to pick me up, I stood at the door for a minute before I opened it. It suddenly hit me that things were different now and I got a little flustered.

I'm someone's girlfriend again.

I opened the door, and he could tell right away that I was in my head.

I don't know how he does it.

I told him I was nervous; he said not to worry and reminded me that I had a birthday toast to look forward to.

Once he knew that I was okay, he told me how much he liked my outfit; though he liked it more when he took it off and found I was naked underneath.

We got there an hour late. We had the edibles, so people were crabby.

Hazel pulled me to the side, I expected that. I told her we would catch up later and I'd tell her everything.

And then I remembered about Max… I didn't see him.

Hazel said he and his brother were running late. I looked at my phone and noticed I never texted him back the other night. Oops.

Hunter and I worked our way through the group, we properly dosed the edible this time and had been sipping drinks here and there.

Max's brother showed up just as Hazel was starting my birthday toast; Max was nowhere in sight. I felt kind of bad for not texting him back earlier in the week, just got distracted.

She brought champagne and had some balloons posted along the way; it was cute!

It was awkward while everyone sang happy birthday, but it was nice of them to do for me; So, I said a few words after and raised a toast to all of them. Hunter kissed me, I know Max's brother saw. I texted Hazel the scoop; well, what I could as a quick update.

A few people decided to start up truth or dare.

Hazel had the first spin, it landed on someone I didn't know very well.

Eventually it landed on Max's brother. He did a dumb dare and spun for his turn. It landed on Hunter.

My heart skipped a beat. I had no idea what was going to happen.

Mind you, it's not like I had done anything wrong, it had been weeks since Max and I slept together.

Hunter chose truth. Max's brother asked him why his last relationship failed.

What a fucking question, right?!

He and I haven't talked about what happened in our previous relationships, so I knew he must have felt a bit uncomfortable. But he answered the question; his previous girlfriend didn't support his career choice and he wasn't willing to give up everything he was working for. She gave him an ultimatum and he chose himself.

He spun the bottle and how cliché, it landed on me. I chose dare.

He had to think about it for a second, but he dared me to say yes until the clock struck midnight. It was only a little after eight, so I had a decent amount of time left ahead of me.

No sooner did Hunter pull me out of that mess of a game.

He grabbed us some bottles of wine and we headed to the room we were staying in and we legit didn't come back out again until we wanted some food.

Thankfully I brought a change of clothes, but more importantly a back up to wear since he exposed my party trick earlier at the house.

I put on a black leather bodysuit; it had a choker and crotchless undies. He was <u>really</u> into it.

He surprised me when he asked me if he could tie me up.

New girlfriend perk unlocked.

We hadn't done that before... but he dared me to say yes until midnight, so that's exactly what I did.

Granted we were both pretty intoxicated, he still made sure I was comfortable.

He tied my wrists above my head, the rest of me was free.

I so wish he had his hat on backwards at the time.

He kissed the center of my chest and moved his way up my neck. He held himself on top of me with just enough of our bodies to be touching for me to feel how hard he was.

As hot as teasing can be, I can only stand so much. He kissed me everywhere, slowly; it drove me fucking nuts. Talk about intense kitty throbbing...

He asked me if I had had enough... I said yes.

He turned me over and fucked me from behind. He asked me if I wanted to try something else, I said yes. But I was in no way resisting. He totally set this up...

He untied me and I got on top of him.

I eventually ended up underneath him and we finished in missionary, believe it or not.

After we got our clothes back on and freshened up, we headed out to grab some food. Everyone was spread out at this point doing their own thing.

We saw Hazel and her boyfriend smoking, as cool as it would have been to join, we didn't, they looked cozy.

We grabbed some food and headed back to our room. By this time, it was close to midnight, and I asked him if he had any last requests before I was able to mouth off again.

We passed a joint back and forth when he asked me if I would tell him how my last relationship ended, so we could be on the same level.

I told him exactly what it was… I felt like I needed to clarify that I just wanted to get my career going before I settled down though.

He very well much understood. He promised me he wouldn't put me in a position where I felt like I had to put my dreams on the back burner. I promised I would support him no matter what he chose to do for work.

The vibe in the room changed.

We made out, then he ate me out while I puffed on the joint and we finished with more sex.

Girlfriend perk for the win.

He eventually fell asleep, and I forced myself to stay awake so I could write. A lot happened today.

I've got to apologize to Max for not texting him back and I need to let him know I can't do the things we used to do anymore.

Entry # 55

SUNDAY SEPTEMBER 1ˢᵀ 2013

WELL, IT'S THE END OF THE SUMMER. I'M SAD BUT ALSO A LITTLE RELIEVED.

I woke up alone this morning and I had a short moment of panic because I thought Hunter ditched me, but a few minutes later he walked in with some coffee.

Dumb on me for assuming the worst and panicking. What a fucking waste of a thought. And why did my mind have to go straight to something negative? I wish I understood why my brain worked this way, I'm working on it.

Hunter went and got us coffee; he figured I needed it just as much as he did. Everyone else was still sleeping, it was a little after eleven. We got ourselves together, cleaned up our room, and headed out.

We needed food in our stomachs, so we stopped for burgers and fries at this random diner. He ran to the bathroom, and I checked my phone for the first time in probably a day.

Scarlett called me for my birthday, I never called her back. Max texted me that he couldn't make it Saturday, but hoped I had a great birthday. I felt bad that I hadn't responded to anyone, I had been with Hunter the whole time.

Mom even texted me to check in and I haven't responded to her yet, either.

I texted Mom back that all was well, and I was heading home soon. I texted Scarlett to see if I could call her today, and Max… I waited to text him back a little later.

Hunter came back and we had a nice lunch. He took me home and walked me to my front door. He called me his girlfriend again. We kissed and went our separate ways. He had an evening shift.

Now that we're dating, living a few doors down from each other is going to make things more interesting.

The parents turned out to be in the back yard, so all was well. I saw them by the pool when I was opening my bedroom blinds.

I took a much-needed shower and plopped right on the couch and started putting pen to paper immediately.

Last night, this entire summer, has been fucking unbelievable.

Shit and tomorrow only starts the beginning of what could possibly be life changing.

From the hours of 9-5 for the next two weeks, I'll be shadowing Mom's job to see if it's a field I want to get into. If after the two weeks it's a good fit for me and I'm a good fit for their team, it'll turn into a permanent position.

I am allowed to not love it, I have been told that this isn't the industry for everyone, so we will see how it goes. I'm staying open minded and I'm excited to learn more about what Mom does for work.

Financial stability is sexy, and I want that for myself.

I will have that for myself.

⦚

I talked to Scarlett on the phone and apologized for missing her; I told her about the surprise party the parents threw and what happened with Austin.

If she didn't know much about him before, she sure does now.

I also told her that Hunter and I are now officially dating, she was so excited for me.

I talked to Max. I apologized for not texting him back earlier in the week, I was honest that I got distracted and wasn't by my phone.

He said he understood and didn't think anything of it.

I told him there was something else I needed to talk to him about.

He asked if it had anything to do with the guy I kissed at the party; of course, his brother reported back. Now, while I didn't owe him a huge explanation, I was going to be respectful.

I was honest, I told him we had been friends since I moved here, one thing led to another, and it turned out that the feelings were mutual so we're going to give it a try.

He didn't mind because he was clear he didn't want a relationship from the start, but he's happy I'm happy. Considering his brother is dating my best friend, we'll probably see a lot of each other so might as well be on good terms.

I felt better getting that out of the way. He was sweet to me, and we had a lot of fun, but we didn't want each other like that. So, it seems like everything has been put to bed.

Looking back on this past summer, I think if I've learned one thing, it's to have fun and live in the moment. Life is short and days are never promised, but also living in the moment can have its consequences.

Back home I was afraid to put myself out there the way I have this summer. Maybe it's easier because nobody knows me around here, regardless, I did what I said I was going to do.

This summer I took my life back, I took my body back, and I chose to live the way I wanted to live, not how someone expected me to.

I don't want to be the person that misses out on moments anymore.

I want fun, I want excitement.

I want to live.

Having Hunter along my side is just a bonus, I still plan to do big things. Maybe he sticks along for the ride, maybe he doesn't. I don't know.

But I do know I'm not going to waste time and obsess over it. I'm going to enjoy what I have in front of me, for as long as I can.

Think about it for a second. I could have moved anywhere in the country, and I just so happened to end up on the same street as my best friends' brothers, friend's house, who turns into my weed dealing boyfriend.

It's just, so peculiar how it all worked out. I guess everything happens for a reason.

Well, hey, on the flipside, I've kept a consistent journal all summer!

I've tried so many times before and it didn't work out, I'm glad my writing is strengthening.

I've taken my life back and now I'm going to take back the remainder of my twenties… I'm going to do my damn best to build a great life for myself down here.

The person I was back home, no longer exists. I may not entirely recognize the girl looking back at me in the mirror right now, but I'm proud of her for not giving up.

I clearly wasn't very happy and considering my surroundings now, I definitely wasn't in the best environment before.

Moving on was the best thing I could have ever done for myself; I feel so much lighter. When you no longer give in to the bad dreams, you know something is going right.

I wish I stopped allowing the wrong people to influence me sooner, but I guess it's good that I know what I know, now.

I still have to cook dinner for tonight, plan my outfits for the week, and get with Mom on my schedule; hence why she reached out to check in… I need to prove to her that I'm serious about job shadowing. These next two weeks are going to be ass husting all day every day.

Also, please buy a new journal; this one is low.

Entry #56

MONDAY SEPTEMBER 2^(ND) 2013

I HUNG OUT WITH MOM ALL DAY; SHE TAKES A LOT OF PHONE CALLS. SHE WAS impressed with the studying I had done previously, and she was intrigued to know that Austin was behind it. Well, she knows I initiated, but you know what I mean.

Between the hours of twelve thirty to one thirty, everyone sits together and has lunch. They make it a priority to keep it up as much as possible when able, since the industry can have its ups and downs.

The fact that Mom manages an entire office staff blows my mind, I had no idea she did so much. She had to rush out for a closing she was attending, so I hung out in her office for the last hour just reviewing my notes and getting myself organized.

Austin stopped in to see how the day had treated me. I was honest and told him it was better than expected because I was prepared, and I thanked him for his help in making that happen. He told me he was an open book and would teach me whatever I wanted to know... I had to remind myself that was about work-related things, and not sex.

It's going to be weird seeing him every day. I don't know if it's guilt for rejecting him or curiosity from rejecting him. Either way, I need to get Austin out of my head.

Hunter had a good first day back to school, though he isn't fond of the schedule, it's manageable and that's all he cares about. His last class ends at four thirty, so he has flex evenings to work, study, or relax, before work on weekends. He graduates in June and is 100% counting down the days.

I'm curious to see where this job shadowing will take me. I may be letting the benefits get to my head, but we'll see. I mean there's nothing wrong with wanting to be successful and I'm not afraid to work. I promised myself I would be open to opportunities, so, it's time to do just that.

Entry #57

TUESDAY WAS RIDICULOUS FOR SOME REASON; EVERYONE'S PHONE WAS GOING off and apparently a borrower refused to sign a document at closing that took three weeks to process. Lunch was not as bright as it was on Monday, I'll leave it at that.

Wednesday was better, they figured out yesterday's issue after hours, so all is well on that front. Mom had to dip out for meetings, so I was stuck sitting with Austin for the rest of the day.

I realized how "adult" this job is… I mean buying a home is the biggest financial decision someone can make in their lifetime, and not all people are in this industry for the right reasons, I've learned. It's a lot of pressure not to fuck anything up, so no wonder it can pay the big bucks.

•••

I ate dinner with Hunter, he made us peperoni and cheese pizzas at his place, his roommate was gone for the night. We ate at the table and drank wine like fancy adults. It was a fun evening, and the kitchen counter sex was an interesting spin on things. Another girlfriend perk I've unlocked.

He was cute, he walked me to my car. As tempting now more than ever to stay the night, it's probably best not to right now with work and school.

I took a hot shower before I climbed into bed. Feeling a little tense, I think it's just because I have to adjust to the office work life. AKA desk job.

Entry # 58

SCARLETT CALLED ME DURING MY LUNCH BREAK, THE MANAGER AT BENJI'S' parents place is leaving, and they need someone to fill in, so Benji hooked her up. I'm excited for her, and I know it'll work out well because she knows what she's doing. To be honest, there was a time long ago I wondered what it would have been like if Benji and I had eventually owned the place and ran it together…

Happy for her.

I got to watch Mom teach a training class and she sounded pretty badass talking about all these different things I don't yet understand; I'm so proud of her.

Today was a very informative day and my brain hurt by the end of it. Mom bailed for a meeting shortly after the training, so I spent the last hour with Austin again. (Hoping this isn't a trend.)

He was sweet, he could tell I had had a day. We went next door and grabbed a drink. He said it's usually what everyone does on Friday, but we could make it an early treat for me given the information overload I had going on.

Austin is a bit of a distraction. He had on a tie today and when he loosened it up, I may have liked what I was seeing. His shirt sleeves were rolled up just enough for you to still see some of the tattoos he has hidden underneath.

Writing this makes me sound horrible. I'm with Hunter, no doubt, no question. I can't believe this is going on in my head right now.

I decided I needed to refocus back to myself, so I thought about creating a morning routine; might as well start the day as best as I possibly can. I found a yoga studio not far from the house with 7am classes, going to give it a shot in the morning.

Hunter had a long day too; he was falling asleep on the phone while we were talking in bed. He sounds so sexy when he's sleepy.

Entry # 59

YOGA WAS GREAT AND I WILL DEFINITELY BE BACK NEXT WEEK. THEY'RE offering a thirty-day free trial so I'm going to give it a try, but I already know I'm going to love it. I'm excited to work on my core and flexibility a bit more. Especially since I haven't been doing it at home like I thought I would.

Oh well.

Job shadowing week one ended not so eventful; I watched compliance videos literally all day so I could learn about mortgage law and history. It was a lot of information.

There was a big storm coming in, so everyone left straight from the office a little before five so we could beat it home.

I went home and took a bath, nothing had started yet, it was just windy out. Hunter video chatted with me when he got off work and just got to his jeep. I teased him with a preview.

He showed up and joined me, we made out and got as handsy as you can in a tub. We moved to the shower. I gave him head and he returned the favor. I guess shower head is another girlfriend perk I've unlocked.

We wrapped up the shower quickly and moved to my bed. We were making out when he suddenly turned me on my side and fucked me with my hair balled in his fist.

Totally came out of nowhere, but I was digging it.

We ordered hibachi for dinner, smoked, and watched a movie in bed. Hunter stayed the night and left early this morning for work.

I went for a ten-mile bike ride and got in one more swim before the parents closed it up for the season. Other than that, it wasn't a bad day, texted with Hunter in between work and went out to dinner with Hazel.

It was nice to catch up without the guys around especially since I haven't really told her about Hunter and me much. Basically, just told her we started out as friends and realized we had feelings for each other and decided to explore them.

After about two hours we parted ways; she went to see Max's brother and I headed home. They are both doing really well by the way. She said it's a bit awkward with Max being the third wheel sometimes, but they get by.

Hunter called me as he was leaving, he had a long day and just wanted to be home.

We hung up so he could shower and yes, he sent a nude. Actually, I think this is the first nude he has sent me now that I think about it.

He called me back and I asked him if he was up for some company, he said yeah but we had to be quiet because his roommate was sleeping.

I drove over there in nothing but my underwear and a jacket long enough to cover me up. He opened the door, and I dropped my jacket exposing my body; I had to return the favor, he sent me a straight up thirst trap earlier.

He was cute, he took me by the hand and walked me to his room, he shut the door behind us and locked it. He had the tv on so there was at least some background noise…

He pinned me against the door, and it was like his hormones just completely took over. He took his shirt off and practically ravished my body; he's a very handsy kisser.

We moved over to his bed and we 69'd for a hot minute, felt amazing. He told me he wanted to be inside me, so we rotated, and I rode him for a minute until he grabbed my hips and started thrusting into me.

My eyes may have rolled in the back of my head because it felt so damn good, he had to shush me, and my mouth was already covered. It was kind of funny- we were giggling, it was cute.

We finished and of course, he finished on my chest. After we cleaned ourselves up, I stayed around and we talked for a few minutes until we called it a night, he had another double to work tomorrow. He walked me out to my car, kissed me goodnight and now you find me here.

It's cool outside right now, so I'm out on the balcony writing, with a joint burning. It's a little after midnight so I know the coast is clear. I'm wearing shorts, a tank top, and a cardigan. So excited for the sweater weather ahead!

Things are going well with Hunter and it's nice hyping each other up about succeeding in what we're doing. I'm glad we can support each other. Not to compare, but to compare, I didn't have that with Benji, he didn't respect that I had a vision for myself and who I wanted to be as a person. He wanted to change my name, I wanted to figure out who I was and make something of myself. I believe now more than ever, that living here is going to help me do just that.

Things happen for a reason and the only way I'm going to get what I want is to start from the bottom and work my way up to the top.

Entry #60

SUNDAY BREAKFAST WITH THE PARENTS WAS AT THIS SUPER CUTE BREAKFAST café. We talked about how the job shadowing was going, and life in general. I almost told them about Hunter, but I decided not to. We're usually pretty open with each other, I'm just not ready to share this with them yet. He and I are too new.

We drove back home together then parted ways. It started raining a little while after they left, so I decided to binge watch romcom movies. I smoked and ended up ordering pizza for dinner; it was delicious, as always.

I'm aware I order pizza often…

Hunter called me, his uncle was closing the place up early so he was wondering if I wanted company.

I mean, without question, yeah.

He picked up some food on the way over and ate at the table while I finished my movie. We moved to my bedroom after and while he was in the bathroom, I took all my clothes off before settling in under the covers.

It didn't take long for him to notice which instantly led to us having sex. We like, appreciated each other's body, and took our time exploring one another before getting nasty… It was hot.

I got on my knees and gave him head. Let's call that, a boyfriend perk he's unlocked.

He managed to get me to stand up and he backed me into the wall and dragged his thumb up and over my lips. He slid his hands down the outer curvature of my body. It was so hot.

He kissed me up and down my neck, then he started to finger me and rub my clit with, you guessed it, the thumb he dragged across my lips; his other hand held him up against the wall. I was totally wet and just dazzled by the dick the entire time. I was living in the moment, and it was fucking awesome.

After he made me cum, we got to the good part and finished with him behind me. He came on my lower back.

I'm getting tired of the cum showers, we have too much sex for him to cum on me. I mean I don't want him to cum in a fucking napkin or something, that's not sexy.

I just don't want him cumming on my body every single time, and I sure as shit don't think it's a good idea for him to cum inside me… then what the fuck is left? Condoms, yeah, but once you've gotten a taste of raw dick, you can't go back. Fuck, I could swallow, but like, no.

Fuck.

Anyway. He spent the night and we made sure we had enough alarms set so neither of us slept in. I had yoga and he had class.

Entry #61

YOGA YESTERDAY WAS FUN! I'M THINKING ABOUT GOING THREE TIMES A WEEK in the mornings before work. Hunter left when I did, thankfully the parents were already gone, but that meant they saw Hunters jeep again. Mom knows, I'm sure she's told Dad. I'll tell them eventually.

Everyone was really busy, the storm had caused some issues regarding inspections, insurance, and appraisals, so everyone was stressed out for most of the day, even had lunch at their desks.

I wasn't sure what to do so I mostly stayed out of the way and helped when I could. Hunter had a good day at school and relaxed for the evening, I think he gamed a little. I read and cooked a nice dinner; made some eggplant parmesan. Used a little too much garlic and herbs, but at least my apartment smelled nice.

Scarlett called me while I was cleaning, and we caught up. She loves working with Benji and his family, and schools' going well, so I'm happy for her. She deserved some fresh air.

Regarding the job shadowing, I haven't talked about it much. I still have questions/curiosities, but so far, I'm leaning towards wanting to take on a position. It seems like a solid career path, not to mention I don't have to put myself into debt to go to college, so there are definitely some perks.

The idea of helping people buy houses seems pretty amazing, too. Makes me feel like I'm doing something good with my life.

Entry #62

THURSDAY SEPTEMBER 12TH 2013

REALLY LOVING YOGA, I THINK I'M GOING TO MAKE THIS MY NEW MORNING routine. It's nice to go out for something other than work, and it's an opportunity to make some new friends.

I spent the day observing, listening, taking more notes, and following different people around. It was exhausting.

Hunter came over for dinner and we organized our notes and studied together. He made us chicken fajitas. The peppers and spices filled my apartment with a spicy aroma.

I love it when he cooks for us, it's so hot.

We had fun quizzing each other, we even made it interesting, if we answered wrong, we either took a shot or took our clothes off. It ended in us naked and tipsy, so we fooled around for a hot minute then took a shower to sober up for the night.

Entry #63

FRIDAY THE 13TH.

Guess who goes to yoga. Austin.

No wonder this place popped up first in my search history; it was the same fucking place he told me about.

He's apparently a regular, he hasn't been in for the last few months because of an injury. So now I see him there and all day at work… awkward. I mean maybe it won't be, after all, we did agree to be each other's accountability partner or whatever.

I spent my final day watching the remaining compliance videos and organizing my notes. Around four, mom brought me into her office, and we discussed how I felt/where my mind was about the industry and overall if I wanted to work there.

She formally offered me a position and I accepted. Monday I officially start as a junior processor. As I learn the industry I can advance, but for now I'll be helping the senior processors get whatever they need. I won't have contact with borrowers, just third-party vendors. I'm excited for this new adventure and opportunity I've been given.

Once the day was over, the entire office went to the bar next door and welcomed me to the team, it was sweet. Not too long after did people start to venture out, Mom included. It was eventually down to Austin and me. We talked about yoga, and he mentioned how much it's helped him in so many ways, and how he's excited for me to get into it.

Once I realized the time, it was about six-fifteen, we parted ways for the weekend.

I went to Hunters place and got an order to go, it was super busy, so I grabbed my food and left.

I went home and romanced myself with dinner, a movie, and a bottle of wine. I drank myself into curiosity, so I took some strong nudes and sent them to Hunter.

As soon as he was let go, he came straight over to my place, didn't waste any time.

I was smoking a joint naked underneath my cardigan when he found me. I was in my room with the balcony door open, there was a calm breeze and it felt nice against my body.

I was feeling really good about myself.

When he walked in, he was wearing a hat, so I turned it backwards and confessed how much of a turn on it is for me. He laughed but took note.

He dropped to his knees and ate me out, while I was still standing there smoking, with his hat on backwards.

After I came and he stood up, I pushed him over to the bed and wet his whistle for a minute or so while he puffed on the joint. Next thing I knew, my legs were over his shoulders with his hand wrapped around my throat and his thumb in my mouth. We had a grip on each other, a grip neither of us were breaking.

And then he came inside me.

I have never sobered up as fast as I did in that very moment.

He apologized, but it was also on me. Granted I was happy to not be covered in cum, I was a little…caught off guard. I cleaned myself up and he offered to drive me to the store for the morning after pill. Since I had technically been drinking, I allowed it.

He was definitely nervous on the drive there, I could tell. I had him chill in the jeep while I ran in.

He was such a gentleman about it, offered to pay and all, but I didn't take his money. I was caught up in the moment too.

I came back out and immediately took it before we headed home. I made him come back inside so he knew I wasn't mad.

We sat on the couch; I straddled him and ran my fingers through his hair while we talked.

I told him that I was tired of being covered in cum, so I wasn't mad about it. He told me I could have told him sooner- blah, blah, blah.

Being that I had just taken the morning after pill, we had one opportunity to really take advantage of it and so, I convinced him to do just that…

We had sex like we were having sex for the first time, it was fucking hot, and it was definitely an odd spin after having to do what we just did. We showered together after, and he spent the night.

Entry #64

SATURDAY SEPTEMBER 14TH 2013

WE SLEPT IN UNTIL ABOUT NINE OR SO. HE MADE US BREAKFAST AND I RAN OUT to get us coffee. When I came home to a man cooking in my kitchen, I giggled walking through the door because I couldn't believe this was my life right now. Leaving him alone in my place was a new level I didn't know we were on yet. I just left; I didn't even think about it until I had walked in on him mid flip with a pancake.

I did my best to not be awkward and ignored that while we ate breakfast on the couch. We talked about plans for the day, he wasn't feeling like going to work, so he texted his uncle and took the night off.

It was a beautiful day, so we decided to go somewhere. We walked the boardwalk, had lunch, and got lost walking up and down the beach. We got away from the crowd and found a lifeguard tower to sit on, so we stuck around and caught the sunset; it was beautiful.

The romance vibes were strong, and I loved every minute of it.

The wind started to pick up, so we made our way back to his jeep. We were so damn close when it started to down pour, and I mean DOWN-POUR, rain came down in buckets.

Got to the jeep soaking wet and somehow that led to me riding his dick in the front seat. I mean nobody could see us because of how hard the rain was falling, so why not take advantage.

We did use a condom this time.

After we finished and the rain lit up, we went back to my place; he dropped me off and went back to his. I showered and munched on some food in the fridge.

Now I'm in bed writing, I've got a joint burning and it's hanging from the corner of my lips.

Makes me feel like an investigative reporter from the old gangster days.

Life is pretty interesting at the moment, and I think now it's safe to say, I'm happy. Scarlett texted me that she's been busy but wants to catch up soon. I am dying to know more of how the restaurant business is treating her now that she's in a management position and no longer a waitress.

Entry # 65

I LIKE TO THINK OF MYSELF AS A POSITIVE PERSON, AT LEAST I DO MY BEST and try.

In my new position as a junior processor, it's my job to order title work, appraisals, homeowners and flood insurance documents, mortgage pay-offs, condo questionnaires, and homeowners' association documents if required. I received a loan on Monday to work, so I did my thing according to the instructions I was given, and I moved right along. Well, the file got to the processor today and upon her review, she noticed the wrong appraisal had been ordered… problem is, the borrowers have already paid and the actual report we need costs an extra $400.

It wasn't a MAJOR mistake; it didn't delay closing and it didn't cause any legal trouble. But it gave the borrowers a bad impression and I feel terrible that happened. Thankfully it was one of Mom's clients and she was able to smooth them over, but just goes to show that training could be a bit better… I now have to work a little more closely with Austin, so we can work together to improve the training program. Given his experience and my lack of, she feels we would make a great team.

I'm excited to help make some positive changes, but overall, I'm kind of fuming.

I was also given "The Speech". Mom explained to me how important details are in this business, and that even the smallest thing could have a huge impact. Don't get me wrong, I totally understand, but if that's the case, why didn't anyone review the instructions I was given?? No one blamed me or pointed fingers at me, but I felt horrible. I felt like I was set up to fail, so I guess it's a good thing I'll be able to help change things, so the next person doesn't feel the way I have.

Couldn't tell you why I'm feeling so hurt by this. I guess its PMS; I should be starting my period any day now. Fucking hormones.

Entry #66

FRIDAY SEPTEMBER 20ᵀᴴ 2013

I WAS IN THE MIDDLE OF YOGA THIS MORNING WHEN MY FUCKING CELL PHONE went off… I forgot to silence it before I went into class. People were not thrilled, but quickly got over it after they saw how embarrassed I was.

As soon as I got out, I had five missed calls from Hazel. She told me her period is over a week late and she's petrified she may be pregnant. Obviously, she and I both had to work for the day so we couldn't do much at that moment, but we did spend the day texting until I could race over after work to check on her. She works from home some days of the week, today was one of those days, so I picked her up and we went to the pharmacy to buy a test together.

She was in such a panic all day… could not imagine that feeling.

We made it back to her house, and I sat on the edge of her bed while she did her thing in the bathroom. She bought two different tests, one digital and one where it shows the lines. She came out and we set a timer for three minutes.

She paced back and forth the entire time in such a panic, I tried my very best to calm her down as much as I could.

Constantly assuring her that I was here for her no matter what was going to happen next.

Well, her test was negative.

Which means she tested too early, or she truly is in fact, not pregnant. It was late in the evening and her doctor's office was closed, so she has no choice but to wait until Monday so she can call her Gyno and get some blood drawn. While she felt some relief seeing a negative test, she was still pretty nervous.

She didn't want to be alone, so I went back to my place and packed an overnight bag. She and I had a sleepover and binge watched sappy romance movies all night after popping some fresh popcorn. Her place smelled because we burned the first batch… but we made it work.

Hunter is sweet by the way. He knew I had a bad day at work yesterday, and while I couldn't share today's details with him, he could tell I was stressed, so he promised to cook me something special for dinner tomorrow night. I'm pretty excited, I love it when he cooks for me.

Side note. I really hope Hazel isn't pregnant.

She's not interested in that right now, and I don't want to see her lose everything she's been working for. Max's brother is great to her, but is he husband/father material?

I know it's not my place or my relationship, but I do care about her, and I want her to be happy. She and I have grown close; I just want the best for her.

Entry # 67

HAZEL GOT HER PERIOD THIS MORNING!!! YES, SHE CALLED ME, AND WE screamed on the phone together, it was great. She wants kids, just not right now.

Anyway. I did not do Sunday breakfast with the parents for obvious reasons… Hunter just left for work, it's shitty outside and I feel like staying in bed today.

I should probably tell the parents about Hunter; I know they see his jeep and I know Mom knows it's his… I just, I don't know.

Dinner last night was extra special. Couldn't tell you specifically why, we just had a really great time together and I wish it didn't have to end. When he came over after work, he had two grocery bags stuffed with food. He knows I love chicken parmesan, so he made me some with his homemade sauce, along with a fresh loaf of garlic bread. My place smelled entirely of garlic, butter, and Italian spices… it was amazing.

When he took out some eggs to bread the chicken, he tried to break an egg between his bicep and forearm like he saw in a video.

Unfortunately, it didn't work out as planned, and egg yolk splattered all over the walls and somehow got on the ceiling! It was hilarious and yes, he did clean it up.

After dinner, we were both feeling pretty full, so we laid in bed and watched a movie; smoked a bowl or two. As I write and read over this entry, it sounds like we had a simple basic night together like we have before, but something just felt different this time. Different in a good way, I just can't seem to put my finger on it.

Maybe it's because we're official and almost a month into dating.

Maybe it's because he made my favorite meal to help me feel better.

Maybe its PMS and hormones.

I don't know, dude. But I do know that I should stop looking into things so much and just enjoy the good things while I have them in front of me.

Speaking of good things.

Hunter used my little vibrating bullet on me while I was giving him head last night.

Not too sure what opened up that can of worms, but I'm certainly down to explore it a little more. It's not like it was out in the open or anything, I was in the middle of doing my thing when he mentioned I should bring it out. I guess using toys in bed is a new girlfriend perk I've unlocked.

…

I got hungry and heated up some leftovers for lunch. Hunters having a crazy day at work so we're not able to talk a whole lot, but it's cool. I sent him a nude or two to make up for it.

Scarlett called me and she is loving management; I knew she would. She seemed to have a little extra… pep in her step… so I'm happy for her, she deserves it. Apparently, it's "awkward" being bossed around by Benji, but otherwise she and him make a great team.

Could Benji be what's making Scarlett so happy? I mean it wouldn't be the worst thing in the world if they got together… but like, why?

Entry # 68

TODAY WAS DAY ONE OF WORKING WITH AUSTIN ON THIS NEW TRAINING procedure he and I are supposed to be creating together. I wonder if he's dating someone because he was wearing cologne that I have not noticed before.

As if he wasn't tempting enough…

It had a fresh, clean, almost aquatic aroma… like he rubbed an ocean smelling bar of soap all over his body. It was very distracting. This "project" of ours better not last long.

Hunter had a bad day with classes and wanted to spend the night gaming, so we did our own thing tonight. I like how we can give each other space to be our own person, I appreciate that as I'm sure he does.

As for myself, I settled on a bubble bath, a face mask, and hair mask; it's been a while since I've done anything.

Side note. The weather is cooling down so I may have to put my bike away for the season. Ugh, going to miss it, but at least yoga's going well, and I have my elliptical that I barely use. Oops.

Speaking of yoga.

It's a little weird seeing Austin there and then at work. Granted I keep my distance at yoga, I can't really do that at work. I wish I knew why I was so drawn to him; I mean it's okay to have friends of the opposite sex, and it's not like we've had sex or anything. But. I do need to put a pin in this lust I have for him before it gets me in trouble.

Entry # 69

BEEN MEANING TO BUY A NEW NOTEBOOK...

It's been two weeks since the new job role and it's definitely the kind of environment that always has you on your toes. Yes, I was stressed recently and questioning whether I wanted this or not, but truthfully this project with Austin has made me realize that I do enjoy the industry, and I think if we had a better training system it could be great; so, I'm excited for the opportunity to make things better for all.

The group chat with the wives has been quiet, so we haven't spoken much since my birthday party. Most of them have kids, so they're dealing with back-to-school life. The girlfriends group has been quiet as well.

Damn do I miss the summer already…

I do need to get something off my chest. My period is almost two weeks late. I did read that the morning after pill could cause a delay… not to mention, I have been under new stress lately; between a new schedule, a new industry to learn, being back in the work force, consistently exercising, and having a man in my life. I'd say that's enough stress in itself to cause a slight delay. Right?

This whole thing makes me want to throw up. I should really go take a test. I guess BRB.

•••

I went to the pharmacy and bought two tests. It says for accurate results to do it first thing in the morning… but I can't wait any longer.

I thought about telling Hunter, but I don't want to worry him for no reason. Scarlett, she wouldn't be able to keep this to herself, now more than ever working alongside Benji.

Hazel… I could technically call her, but I think I want to be alone when I find out. I'm honestly scared because I'm not ready for this, nor do I want it right now.

I don't know what to do, I mean, there's always Mom I could go to. But she may tell Dad, and her knowing is enough to deal with, let alone him, too.

I'm running out of room on the page. I just set the timer for three minutes.

•••

What if the test is positive? This is literally why Benji, and I broke up… This can't be happening.

Fuck. I don't know what I'm going to do.

I just got control back and I'm finally happy, like truly happy. We only slipped once, and I took the morning after pill like right after. Yeah, we took advantage, but like, I'm also on birth control, I take that shit like clockwork.

One test was positive, the other was negative. I have no idea which one I peed on first. Whatthefuckdoido?

Acknowledgments

First, I want to thank my beta readers for all of their guidance and patience as I navigated the anxiety of sharing my work publicly for the first time. I truly thank each of you for your support.

To my husband, Tim.
Throughout our years together, you've always believed in me, even when I couldn't myself. Thank you for always supporting me in every way to finish this book, and for understanding how important writing is to me. Your love and support means the world to me. I love you so much.

To the publishing team at Palmetto Publishing, thank you for putting up with all my crazy questions and most importantly, turning my dream into a reality.

Lastly, I want to selfishly give a shout out to my younger self. I thank you for never giving up. You managed to keep writing through it all, and that is why today, you are officially a published author.

You did it ❤